Sanitarium Magazine
Issue no. 49

Thank you to all of our contributors, we couldn't have done it without you.

FACULTY MEMBERS

Dr. Sputnik
Dr. Muratori
Dr. Soldan
Dr. Algee
Dr. Marceau
Dr. Warra

Contents

Issue Forty-Nine
Dedication

Each and every writer who appears in Sanitarium is special to us.

This reprint of issue 49 is dedicated to the memory of Mary Renzi, who sadly lost her long battle with cancer on 11th January 2021.

Leaving our marks (large & small) on the world is important to all of us. Sanitarium is honoured that one of Mary's will forever be included within this issue.

My heartfelt condolences go out to Mary's family.

Ian Sputnik
Editor

It's horrible to hear when we lose one of the Sanitarium family. During my tenure, we had marriages, births and other celebratory accomplishments - but death always hits hard.

I'd like to extend my condolences to Mary's family

Barry Skelhorn
Founder and former Editor of Sanitarium Magazine

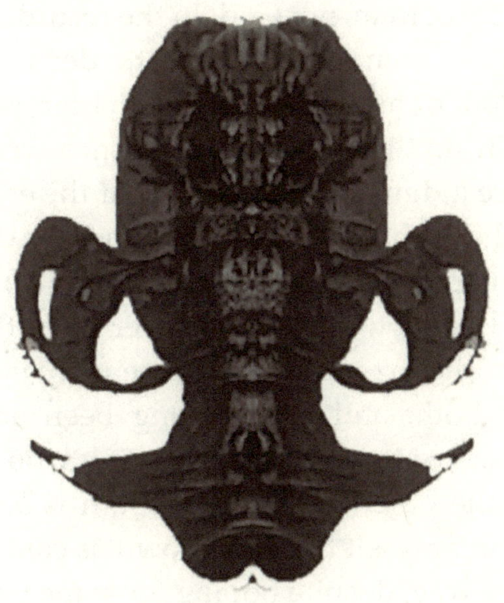

For We Are Many by Gregory Owen

As a man of science, I am expected by my colleagues to disregard my faith in the powers beyond scientific explanation. I am expected to only follow the gospels of quantum physics, orbital mechanics, genetic engineering, deductive reasoning- that is, the endeavors of Man, not God. In the recorded past, to believe one or the other compelled others to deem you an outcast. Believers in God, or any deity for that matter, were ridiculed for placing faith in myths; believers in science were told that they would embrace judgment upon arrival at the end.

But things have changed very little since the discovery of deep space travel and planetary colonization, and I do not comply with expectations. I cannot. I am a follower of both beliefs, a man lingering upon the razor's edge between two systems but never submitting to both, and I have long been an outcast in the presence of peers, yet much more than any who commit to either path. One or the other, never both- both is *blasphemy*! I never enjoyed devoting myself to every crowd as conformity was not a prerogative anyway, despite hoping for some form of belonging- some form of communion. I needed something to follow. I had to rebel somewhere; I would tell myself. I was a scientist holding a crucifix. An oxymoron. Even as a senior biologist for Her Majesty's Ship *Ozymandias*, I am treated with some form of skepticism. For the sake of argument, though, I can claim science as the source from which I extract my communion more often than not.

However, when our shuttle's navigation systems detected a hull breach, caused by tiny pieces of impetuous debris outside of the planet's thin atmosphere (undetected by our imperfect, non-preemptive sensors- damn it all), I ignored the Lord of Equations and Reasoning. When our orbit began to decay at a frightening pace, I prayed for something to save us, something beyond science and fact, screaming my pleas as we crashed. I prayed for Doctor Nix and Lieutenant Galen, and for myself- for our very survival.

Now, floating in darkness, my testimony is currently being recorded for a tribunal representing the Coalition for Allied Planetary Exploration, and, more than I can bear, I wish I had never uttered any such prayer on that descent. I pray that I never had and that maybe, just maybe, this has all been hallucination, but I know differently. The analytical portion of my brain knows differently, and will not be denied. Some*thing* did hear my insignificant prayers, and it had nothing resembling salvation in mind.

"Doctor Jacobs," says Commandant Eckers, her voice droning in a mechanically firm tone. "We need to know what happened on the surface of TNG-982." She booms through wherever I am, and the noise echoes throughout my containment as though I am within a soulless womb, all other senses dulled by deprivation.

Of course, *they* need to know. A reconnaissance endeavor failed, a PEV-12 (Planetary Exploration Vehicle) valued at 6.2 million pounds was destroyed, two crewmen are dead, and the only remnant of it all is me. *They need to know.* I cannot claim that I know for sure anything truly relevant- all that I do know is that TNG-982 is dangerous, enough to drive a stable man like myself mad and change him. According to the good Commandant, upon retrieval by the Ozymandias, I was a raving lunatic coated in blood, peeled out of my suit and clutching my crucifix necklace, hoping, but knowing, that no comfort would be provided ever again. Not with the knowledge given to me, still embedded, planted deep within my cerebral cortex. Taken onto the ship (I am still uncertain just *how* I was rescued as the moments between the loss of my team and my arrival on the Ozymandias are fleeting images, sounds, and smells now, at best), I was sedated, though I struggled viciously.

In the absence of sanity, an animal's first instinct is to fight, and fight I did. Eckers tells me that the four men who rescued me had to restrain me, suffering multiple contusions, a concussion, a fractured clavicle, and two shattered elbows; which one suffered which is unclear. The stinging ache of my own muscles suggests that the crewmembers with whom I did battle were not the only among the wounded. They just happen to be in the infirmary while I'm here, wherever *here* is.

"You did these things while screaming that the planet was dangerous and would kill us all," Eckers continues, "And you kept saying the words "*communion*" and something that sounded like "*lesion*." Do you recall?"

"No," I answer with confidence, for I truly did not have memory of saying or doing those things.

"What did you mean?" she asks methodically.

"I don't know. I-" I don't remember uttering any such words, nor do I remember my return's struggles, but I do recognize the words. I know what I meant- my momentary lapse into madness did not erase from my mind the meaning, only the occasion. I heard those words often on the planet's surface. My memories flood my synapses, and they flow into my mouth like bile, spewing forth in words. "*Legion*," I whisper. Then a realization reveals itself in an empty zone of my cognition. It explodes like a round from a CAPE-issued pulse rifle. "Did anyone onboard come to the surface?"

"Yes."

"My God. How-?" How did anyone on that team survive? What if they're no longer who they were?

"The PEV was utterly destroyed. There was no other way to get to any of you. Transmissions had failed, so Captain Tyrell...violated protocol...to save you." Eckers inhales softly, though it fails to subdue the disdain apparent in her tone. "He believed you and the rest of your team were more valuable than any equipment owned by the CAPE. I only authorized your team to go because of its size and Lieutenant Galen's combat experience, seeing as how the Ozymandias has operated on a skeleton crew due to our dwindling budget as it is, and then he decides to send a rescue team to the last known point of contact in another PEV." Her pregnant pause only indicates annoyance. "But...luckily for you, you were not far away, and they brought you back immediately. So I-*we*-need to understand what transpired and assess the situation to determine exactly what occurred on TNG-982."

The good captain, Malcolm Tyrell, values his crew- values us, values me. He has been one of the only people on this bothersome vessel to make me feel as though I belonged to something greater, something above my outlooks and beliefs. The only other is Doctor Andrea Nix. *Was* Doctor Andrea Nix.

"You must examine the rescue team, keep them quarantined like me!" Good Captain Tyrell sent more crewmen to the surface, the fool! My only fear is that he has made a grave error in judgment, one that carries with it implications of a most horrifying nature. Damn his "leave no one behind" philosophy! Damn us all! There are things that exist in the vastness of time and space not meant to be known by Man, and among the celestial bodies I've touched under my feet, this is the first I've determined is uninhabitable, and with good reason.

"Why?"

"Just do it! I-" *Christ!* The ache inside becomes terrible pain, and it increases deep in the sinew of my musculature, allowing me to only grunt in discomfort. A horrid spark trickles all through me as though my blood carries with it seething fire. My stomach churns and bubbles, and nausea manifests.

"Doctor Jacobs, are you all right?"

I cannot see, but I grip my arm, what seems to be the source of the agony, and feel the lumpy scar: a wound I know that I received on TNG-982. The one given to me by Edward Galen, CAPE Lieutenant- only, it wasn't *Galen*.

A white-hot searchlight explodes the room and blinds me. "Yes, you were wounded when we found you," Eckers mutters, seeing that I'm clutching my arm. "Aside from minor abrasions- cuts, bruises- and beyond the blood, that wound is all that we found. Nasty, from the looks of it. Like an animal's scratch."

With her observation compounded on to my own, I formulate an answer, the same one that I hypothesized when I received the wound:

Contagion.

Slow, but all-consuming, infection.

Nix and Galen were attacked outright, murdered and altered, but me- I escaped with a scratch. It was but a tiny door, one through which *it* entered and established residence. *It* spoke to me. Why can I not hear it now? It provided the knowledge I will have to use to convince Eckers, and save others from what might come. Even as an expert in biology, both human and extra-terrestrial (though much of the alien life discovered has been of the microscopic, single-celled variety), I do not know nor comprehend every single detail, every process, involved in what I witnessed. But I know just enough.

"You seem to be healing rather quickly," Eckers continues, "and that should be considered a small miracle, too. But no matter. Now for the task at hand."

I attempt to see beyond the light, to see a face looking back, but there isn't one to be found. Eckers, for all I know, is behind me, above me, underneath me; I'm praying that she's behind one of the walls, away from me. I have to remain in this isolation tank for the safety of the Ozymandias. "I'll tell you what happened, Commandant. But you must promise me something."

"No promises, Doctor. But I will do what is necessary once we're finished."

I remain adamant in my negotiation, despite knowing that withholding my testimony will inadvertently yield destructive consequences. "No. You either agree to what I ask, or I say nothing."

"You have nothing to negotiate, Doctor Jacobs," she says stoically. "This is merely to ascertain what occurred on your mission and to determine your state of mind. CAPE needs your information, however, and we would rather obtain it willingly, especially now that you at least *appear* stable."

"Please," I ask.

The searchlight clicks, and I am once more enveloped in the dark. A moment of silence, and then Eckers speaks. "Very well. Go on."

"Keep the rescue team quarantined," I say again.

A brief silence, until Eckers finally replies, "It will take time. I am to interview them once they have concluded tests in the infirmary, and once we're finished with your debriefing."

"Do it now," I demand.

"Fine." No words for the moment, as I am sure she is debating with someone nearby, or over comms, about the rescue team. I just hope that she heeds that warning, as well as the ones coming. "Continue," she says.

"Do not return to TNG-982. No one must ever go there- tell Tyrell," my bones scorch and crackle with needles, "tell him to *destroy* it if he can. One of the War Freighters can do it. They're equipped with surface-piercing thermonuclear missiles, yes?" The scar on my arm begins to itch and the surrounding skin prickles into gooseflesh. "And do not, under any circumstances, retrieve anything else from the surface-"

"But Doctor Jacobs-"

"*Listen, damn you*! Don't! No bodies, no wreckage, no samples- nothing!" I breathe deeply in an attempt to regain myself. "And lastly, once I'm finished telling you what happened..." I trail off, finding that I'm scratching harder and harder upon the scar, my nails already peeling away the surface of the fresh skin.

"Doctor Jacobs..."

"When I'm finished..." Beneath the skin, among the muscle tissue of my forearm, something stirs, sending a pulse through my mortal being. It reawakens. "*You must kill me, and incinerate the remains.*"

She relents. After a moment, I begin my account, and Commandant Eckers begins recording.

Consciousness returned at nightfall, its only solace being that it ended my fiery nightmares of the crash itself. I deduced that my prayers for the survival of my team were successful when I saw that both Doctor Nix and Lieutenant Galen were up and about, having pulled me away from the PEV-12's gnarled wreckage. I noticed that my helmet's HUD read "O2 Levels Optimal," though I neglected to remove it regardless of the atmosphere's breathability. We were still unsure of any potential airborne pathogens, and I saw that both Nix and Galen had kept theirs on. I silently thanked God, feeling that anything else would have allowed our deaths, and I pushed myself up to examine the surroundings.

For a seemingly dead planet in a seemingly dead solar system, I was amazed days earlier when the Ozymandias's sensors acknowledged a large carbon-based presence. Immediately, I asked that I be included in the small recon team to be sent to explore the planet, codenamed TNG-982, and I was excited at the prospect of observing and discovering new life. I didn't even mind that I would only be accompanied by one CAPE soldier to deal with the very idea of possible danger- I only cared about exploration. Yet in the aftermath of impact on the surface, standing in the opacity of the night air, I found that the land around me was devoid of life. Gripping some loose soil in my hands was like sifting through cold ash. It had all been for nothing.

"...All for nothing," I mumbled.

"Lieutenant! He's conscious!" It was a moment before I realized that it was Nix speaking, and that she was talking about me. Her hurried footsteps crunching toward me snapped me out of my trance. "Oh God, Trevor, are you all right?" The amount of gladness in Andrea Nix's eyes gave just the tiniest bit of comfort, but I detected the anxiety there too, and I shared it with her. *I wanted to share better things with her.*

"Y-yes, I'm fine, Andrea. Are you okay?"

"I am, Trevor." Her cheeks briefly flushed, and she helped me to my feet. "You were unconscious after the crash," she continued. "I wasn't sure whether or not you were in any form of a coma. It's not my expertise, you know." It was true- she was a botanist, a student of the sister science to my own, though she deemed herself a "xenobotanist" due to the fact that in terms of alien life, plants had been discovered in more abundance and studied with much more scrutiny. We had always held something of a friendly rivalry during our time on the Ozymandias, and she was most certainly in the lead in the contest of discovery. I had something to prove, though this planet was proving to be yet another dry spot for me. "But you seem fine to me," she finished reassuringly, gently touching my shoulder.

"Goddamn CAPE equipment!" I recognized the steely, dryly American growl of Lieutenant Edward Galen, and fully understood his frustration. Even when he spoke, however, he still sounded abnormally calm.

"What is it, Lieutenant?" I asked.

"Pay for perfection, get sub-par, that's what. Fucking budget cuts." He came over to us, seething as he tossed a piece of scrap into a pile littered with wires and electronics from the inside of the PEV-12. "Glad to see you up and about, Doctor Jacobs. You weren't looking especially well when we landed-" He paused to correct himself. "*Crashed.*"

I withdrew as the chaotic descent's memory filled me with flashing crimson lights and the claustrophobic wheezes induced by the belief that death was fast approaching. Beyond his visor, I saw the concern in Galen's eyes as I recalled the moments leading to the crash, and I did my damnedest to stifle the trauma. However, in his eyes, dwelling behind that façade of strict, calculating military training, I could also see the smallest hint of fear embedded- concealed, though not quite hidden. "Are you all right, Doctor?"

"Yes," I managed.

He cleared his throat, likely trying to conceal his anxieties in a similar fashion as to my own, and was back to business. "Okay, then. Doctor Nix, see if you can find me any materials to fashion a radio, a beacon, something. We have to alert the Ozymandias so they can send a rescue team."

"They- they may already know something's wrong," I said.

Galen wasn't buying my idea. "Maybe they have, but I'm not taking that chance. They may think we're dead." He began walking past Nix and me, his footsteps crunching along the ground like hammers on shattered glass. "There's more wreckage nearby," he said, pointing at a dimly lit area a few meters away. "I'll comb through it. You two can do one last sweep here. Put whatever you find in that pile."

"Right," Nix replied. "C'mon, Trevor."

I nodded, but felt a sudden tremor below me. We all felt it. The ground beneath Lieutenant Galen shifted and moved. He fell to his knees, landing heavily, and the rumbling caused me to drop as well.

Nix maintained her balance and reached down for me. "What in the hell is going on?"

I had no idea, and I could see in Galen's shocked face that he didn't, either. "Galen! Galen, are you all right?"

But he was unable to reply before what came next. From the alien earth below him, something resembling a spiny tentacle erupted upward and loomed above. As he started to cry out for help, the limb whipped around Galen's head and clenched, crushing the reinforced glass of his helmet into his face. The broken chunks splintered and fell apart, and the tentacle drilled its clicking claws into his skull, shredding and slicing away in sticky strips.

Grasping a shard from his helmet's remains, Galen jabbed the monstrous thing desperately. It recoiled with an inhuman shriek, surrendering its grip on the CAPE soldier, rising up as it dropped him clumsily to the dirt. Galen lumbered weakly, clutching his ruined head in his hands like a bushel of apples, fearful that juicy pieces would scatter should he relinquish his hold. Ruby red pulp flowed from his ears onto his shoulders, staining the charcoal suit a dull, sticky maroon.

"*Runnnn,*" Galen garbled through pulverized lips. He crawled only a few feet and collapsed, prompting Nix in her window of adrenaline-fueled clarity to want to sprint toward him, though I knew that he would not survive the injury, regardless of whether she saved him or not. It didn't take a biologist to determine that.

The tentacle, meanwhile, became a rigid column of slimy meat and pulsed violently, erupting into a mass of multiple, unique organisms. Each was the size of a small dog but all had various limbs, arachnoid and crustacean in appearance, squalling mouths and wagging tongues- all of the creatures were differently shaped and moving outward like an ocean wave. I grabbed Nix's leg to prevent her from running headlong into the mass, telling her that it was of no use and that we needed to avoid detection or else we suffer Galen's fate. She defiantly tried to pull me, but upon hearing Galen's gurgling moans, she resigned her efforts- she knew I was right.

Within seconds, they were all upon him, latching on and consuming his body. His dwindled shape thrashed in agony, but while a great number of the creatures scuttled back toward the hole from which they appeared as part of the tentacle, some remained behind and began fusing themselves onto Galen. It seemed as though they were adding biomass to his remains, altering him: Parasites changing him at a cellular level, providing him with nutrients, reconstituting his shape into something gnarled, malformed...*terrifying*.

By God, I had never seen anything like it in nature, not on Earth or anywhere else. What kind of organisms were these things? What were they doing? Were they making him predatory? Could they have been weaponizing him?

It was horrible to witness as a God-fearing man, but fascinating from the view of my biologist's eyes- no, dare I say it, my *xenobiologist's* eyes! To see a beast of such terrible majesty, something so horrific and unlike anything studied on Earth, on any planet within our dominion thus far, left me in silent awe, a feeling interrupted only by the pleading of my colleague. "Trevor, we need to go! Come on!" She was right, though my judgment lapsed in favor of more study.

When Galen shifted and stood, I did the same, slowly, and Nix continued tugging my arm. Only when the creature, an amalgam of assorted claws and tendrils fused by slimy veins of flesh, turned to face me did I fully comprehend the immediacy of the danger, and my God-fearing half wrestled control from morbid curiosity. Still, it was too late and I was frozen, locked in place by nothing more than shivering fright. "Damn it, Trevor, come on!" Nix screamed, releasing me and moving away behind me, expecting me to follow suit. But I was unable.

The monstrosity that wore the malformed visage of Edward Galen shambled toward me like a puppet held by invisible strings, its motor functions jumpstarted by jolts of some unknown power that caused jerking, irregular motions. It came faster and faster, reaching for me with squirming appendages no longer appearing as human hands, but more like bouquets of assorted, bony fingers. I could feel the instinct of flight returning, but I only managed to lift my arms before the grotesque beast had me by my wrists.

"Galen, no..." I managed.

Gasping from behind my helmet's visor, comprised of reinforced glass that acted as the only protection separating me from the creature, I then tried to scream for Nix. I gazed at its horrid appearance as I struggled, all of its features aglow in the orange light of the PEV-12's nearby blazing wreck. The only quality remaining of Galen upon the abhorrent form that, only moments before, had been his head was his stern, dark face. He stared at me, his dead, pearlescent eyes glaring into mine and beyond- nothing recognizably human dwelled behind them- and small growths, like boils, breached his cheeks and forehead. His mouth opened and released a roar that sounded nothing like the calm modality of Edward Galen's speech, rising higher in pitch until it was a shriek, and my breaths came quicker and quicker as I saw the boils swell, forming fissures that began rippling and tearing apart. Like a flower, Galen's face spurt outward, splitting open in uneven pieces. Each petal produced teeth that sprayed translucent ooze and coated my visor.

"Nix, help me!" I tried helplessly to pull away, but its strength was unmatched by my own. From the thing's maw came Galen's tongue, swelling like a balloon until it burst, metamorphosing into a cluster of tiny, fork-like hands that reached out and clutched my helmet. "Nix!" I cried as my head was enveloped.

The grip on my arms suddenly released, dropping me to the ground, and I opened my eyes. The Galen-creature yelped and, through the gooey smear on my visor, I witnessed a blurred Nix attacking it, beating it senseless with a titanium rod coated in fiery fuel from the PEV-12. It screeched in anguish; each wail punctuated by a muted clang of metal upon flesh. In moments, the only noises I could hear above my wheezing breaths were Nix's grunting and the crackling of flames- the attack had set the alien thing ablaze. It attempted to escape, but Nix pursued, wanting to put an end to the threat.

"Andrea!" I shouted, only hearing the primal shrieks of the creature. I wiped away the beast's saliva to see more clearly, and it was then that I felt a sensation of growing discomfort. There was something in my arm, and I knew immediately: a claw from the Galen-creature's malformed hand had scratched open the arm of my suit, lodging itself in the muscle of my forearm, and it was still twitching.

Oh God! Contagion! My insides quivered in panic, and denial could not quell my terror. Nothing could.

I had borne witness to what a life-form on this planet could do to a perfectly healthy human being when attacked, and I shuddered at the prospect of what could happen to me- no, I wasn't being overwhelmed by an army of creatures, but just one open wound could bring about potentially gruesome results. All hope was dashed, scattering like a deck of cards in a blast of icy air, for the biologist within knew that this was it. God would not be able to save me here.

There was still the matter of the thorny digit sticking from me, still affected by the spasms brought on by recent, traumatic injury, a reaction strangely akin to homo-sapiens; perhaps we had much more in common with these alien beings that comprehension granted. Its damage was surely done, and there was no telling what effect it would have on me, but I could at least be comfortable. I reached for it, but it moved away. It *sensed* my action. It knew, and in a bid for self-preservation, the parasitic thing tore itself deeper into my skin.

The moment that it carved into my muscle tissue, my nerves screamed and I followed suit. I felt it move up my bicep and into my shoulder, and though the agonizing sensation lessened, muted perhaps by the abundance of muscle and organic tissue surrounding it as it moved deeper into my body, I could still feel it. A dull, throbbing ache made its way through my chest, passing my lungs and stomach, and moved toward my spine, continuing its passage upward. Upward toward my-

Noise flowed into my ears, but I realized that I wasn't actually hearing it. It was- it was only in my head. It was telepathic in nature.

It began as a hum, and its vibrations snaked across my skull in tingling waves, growing louder until I could feel my brain crackling with the volume of indeterminable wails, none of them belonging to anything on Earth. I could only wince in anguish, my cranium becoming white-hot, so much more excruciating than Galen's talon moving inside of me, and then and there, I wanted to die. I begged for an end. I wanted God to end it!

Something else heard, however, for within moments, the roars shifted. My silent pleas were understood. The noises pitched lower and were as moans, and the group of sounds intertwined into one, beastly tone.

The voice spoke. *"Doooc...toorrrr..."*

The idea of telepathy was then confirmed to me. It, the source of the sound, had scanned my mind, likely learned- *taught itself-* the English language. Everything I'd learned from youth to my time at Oxford, all of it. Communication was made simpler for the both of us. Words that wanted to grace my lips first danced across my mind.

Oh my God, I thought.

"Nooo...*thing* existsss here...like yooour *'God.'"

Telepathy was confirmed further. I had no reason to speak anymore.

What...what are you?

"You?" it gurgled with a surly, almost pompous sound. **"*I am we.* There is not *one*, but *we* are *one*."**

Hearing the voice's words, I was reminded of a Biblical quote I remembered reading in youth. *Mark 5:9.* I could see it as though I were sitting at home as a teenager, reading it from my father's ornately decorated King James Bible.

The voice hissed, and it realized which quote I was recalling, stating it in a clearer, more enunciated pattern than what I heard moments before. Its speech was improving. **"*I am Legion. For we are many.*"** I detected a satisfied growl in the creature's tone. **"Yes. *We are one. I am all.*"**

I was completely dumbfounded. All of this time I had spent in trying to discover new, extra-terrestrial life, and had found nothing beyond microbes and bacterium, and now, now, a life-form had destroyed Lieutenant Edward Galen and was now communicating with me *telepathically*! Leaps and bounds beyond what I expected, to be sure! Oh God, was I really feeling intrigued? I had to know more. I had so many questions, and I'm sure it could hear them all. What else could I do but 'talk'? I'd die anyway, or become some monstrous thing at the least.

How long have you been here?

"I have been for cycles that are countless. I bore witness to the beginnings and endings of many beings. This orb is not my

only dwelling. I am many. This place contains only a piece of me, one not lost to time, carried by the winds of many suns."

Just...a piece?

"Yes. But I am whole. I share one voice comprised of many. This part of my being slept. This system was extinguished, its light dampened out from time. I had to wait. I waited inside, as I did when the life here was not part of my *congregation*."

Upon hearing that utterance of the word "congregation," I felt as though I were sitting in church with my parents as a child. The creature's voice had adopted the volume and confidence of a priest. I almost *admired* it. And then, a revelation burst into my consciousness: it's a life-form hidden within a dead shell! The source of the carbon-based presence in the Ozymandias' scans-this thing, a hostile organism trying to communicate civility to me, was the planet itself! Madness!

"Yes," it replied, seizing my mental divulgence. "The life was sustenance for a mere cycle and ceased once the *communion* was complete. It joined me, I brought it all with me here. Inside. So I slept. Then *you* came."

Communion? What do you know of communion?

"I know what you know. I briefly misunderstood its meaning until I swallowed deeply your knowledge. It is what we offer. *Communion*."

You don't offer 'communion!' You offer pestilence! Disease! Death! I saw what you did to Galen, you fucking monster!

The voice groaned. "You insignificant beings are curious. Edward Galen had no time to converse with me as you do. His noises were screams. Brought me pain...such agony. Still screams." I was sure the alien was alluding to the brutal beating Nix was giving the Galen-creature, though I could no longer hear anything beyond its voice.

"But you," it continued. "You think me a virus, Doctor, and while I am not completely unlike one, the same can be said for what you *all* are, as well- what all species I've tasted are." My brain squirmed as the being's influence pierced needles deeply into each lobe, as though forcing me to submit to its argument. "I see what you have seen. What you know. You are each a conscious disease. You only serve your own individual purposes, fighting, destroying. You infect, breed, grow, consume, and spread. *I offer union.* You are afraid and you reject it. Already, I have tasted your kind and for such complex formations of multiple cells, you are so crude elsewhere. I swallow, I digest, I change. I improve. *I improve you.* I give you all of the life I have sampled throughout time, the abilities to have them, to show and utilize them, just as you will give me. I grant the communion that I know you crave, Trevor Jacobs."

Its hold relinquished slightly, allowing me to gather myself enough to form cohesive thoughts, but just barely. *I-I don't want this! You made Galen an...an abomination! I can't become one myself!*

"I will allow you to regain yourself, just as he would have. Your current form. You will not be totally destroyed."

He only resembled Edward Galen. He wouldn't be him. *I won't be* me!

"You will be in your image, but also my image. All images are mine. His memories will be swallowed into mine- ours- all that have been collected. Your memories will be part of the collective."

Not if I destroy myself...

"You will not. Your beliefs will not allow it. You feel that your *salvation* will elude you if you commit suicide."

I'm no longer...human. Or I won't be much longer. Not with this...thing, this cancer...in me... If I did, I wouldn't be taking a human life. My human life.

The being sounded amused. "But you are afraid, too afraid to do so. It is a sensation I have tasted before, and I have never forgotten. *I have missed it.* You are unsure of what comes after. You claim to believe that you will have life beyond this shell bestowed by your *God.* Accept the communion, Trevor Jacobs. Join our congregation. Experience what we provide. You will have everlasting life, be many. Be all. Be *Legion.*"

As if I have a choice! I closed my eyes, bringing warm tears, attempting to deny my terrible fate. But over TNG-982's voice, I heard another coming in labored breaths. "I...I killed it, Trevor."

"I have grown weary of remaining here," the thing continued. **"I want to experience more. I want to experience more of *your* kind. More of the kinds beyond this derelict system."**

"Trevor, are you all right? I said I killed it!" It was Andrea Nix. She couldn't hear what I did. "Whatever Galen *was*...it's dead..."

"More," it said. **"I will experience *this one*."**

"No!" I managed hoarsely. "No, you won't!" It took all of my strength to combat the creature's influence, though maybe it simply allowed me to win and its voice ceased, if only for a moment. "No!"

"What? Trevor, come on, get up! We need to do what...Galen wanted. We need help!" She reached down, tugging at my shoulders in an effort to lift me.

"No," I said. "Andrea, please. Leave me. I'm...I'm infected... It's in me...I can *hear* it."

She was not to be denied and continued in vain. "Come on, Trevor. I won't let you die here!"

"No! Look!" I presented my arm, showing her my bloodied wound. "Galen did this- you saw what those things can do. It's changing me inside!"

"But-!"

"Contagion, Andrea! You quarantine contagion! I'm a threat to you and everyone else...Leave me!"

She ceased and leaned close, her eyes glimmering wet and wide in the light of the fire behind her visor. "No, I won't let you! I want you to come back with me! I-!" She paused, still unable to earn a breath. Behind her, I sensed some movement, but felt it to be a trick of my weakened eyes and mind. Deep within my subconscious, however, I knew what it was. I knew. I knew the futility of everything, too- the futility of saving myself, of convincing Andrea to leave, of identifying the long, twisting form extending from the earth below only meters away. The only futility of which I wasn't aware at that time was in saving her.

I learned quickly, though. "Listen, Andrea, I know...I *care* about you, too..." She smiled ever so briefly. I wished that I could have touched her cheek, feel its warmth. "But you're in grave danger. I know what it is, the life form here! What it wants!"

"**Communion**," the alien thing said, its voice returning.

"It will assimilate all it touches! It's doing it to me! It will to you, too... I cannot leave!"

At the end of the long, twisting form, what the flame's light revealed to be a tentacle belonging to TNG-982, an organic javelin formed. "**And neither can she...**"

"Andrea! No-!" I cried. She never knew it was coming.

In that instant, a cloud of blood sprayed onto the ground and all over me, and Nix's chest was flayed open like a mouth, the javelin curling into a hook that ensnared its prey like a fish on the line. Nix begged, pleaded, and reached for my hand as if I could save her. "Trevor!" Her words were turning into moist gurgles. "Trevor, please-!" The organic hook twitched and quickly merged deeper within her, forcing the killing tip through her visor in a glassy crunch, effectively entering her mouth and piercing the back of her skull. She was forcibly jerked into waiting the darkness below the surface.

Another for the flock, I thought bleakly. I wanted to laugh, and I believe that I did for a moment before weeping. I wept for Nix, for Galen...for me. For what seemed an unbearable eternity, I wept and I waited. I waited to die, to be taken and horribly ripped apart, to be made into a new organism. I waited for the severed appendage inside to consume me. I waited for the tentacle that took Nix to finish me. I waited for one of the multiple organisms that changed Galen to come for me. Something. But nothing came except for one last statement from the monstrous alien. "**Doctor Andrea Nix- A new member of our congregation. And you will join her, Trevor Jacobs.**"

It was then that I felt that the creature wanted my change, my metamorphosis, to be slow. To let me suffer. It had quickly taken Galen and Nix, but why not me? What was my reason for remaining? It had to be that it wanted me to endure the torture of the passage of time as infection consumed me. I was sure that having "tasted" humankind, the creature had already learned the little touch of evil inherent only to us: *cruelty*.

I waited, thoughts of oblivion and what lied beyond for me, my impending loss of humanity, the existence of this intelligent being within the planet and its past, what created it, the possibility of whether or not there was indeed a God as I had known Him, and on and on- nothing came but a swirling deluge of madness followed by unconsciousness...that is, until I was awakened by the roar of propulsion from a rescue craft and the madness returned in force.

"And you already know the circumstances regarding how I came aboard," I finish, concluding my account.

"Is that everything?" Commandant Eckers asks.

"Yes. That's all of it. And now you can fulfill what you promised me."

"Because of *contagion*, correct?"

"Yes, Commandant, and something else." An epiphany has revealed itself in my retelling of events, and it makes perfect sense now in the painful fire of my cognizance. I recall what the being said, and I know why it didn't immediately assimilate me when it had the chance.

I want to experience more.

A virus spreads when it escapes containment, seeking to infect and grow, as science teaches us. That's why I escaped. It wants the ship- that way, it can go anywhere. The craft will become a hypodermic to carry and inject this disease into any planetary host, a spore to hold with it the destruction of all sentient life. "That *thing* in TNG-982 will assimilate every living thing it encounters, including the crew of the Ozymandias. And because...*it's inside of me*...I *have* to be destroyed..." A jolt flushes through me and every piece of me burns, the pain of my change returning. "Christ!"

"Experiencing discomfort, Doctor Jacobs?" The searchlight clicks on, and Eckers is mechanical, completely unconcerned with my plight. She should be.

I struggle to maintain myself and my composure, even as the pain becomes unbearable. "You...er, you contained the rescue team...correct?"

"Yes."

"I hope so. I...I truly do. Ah...now, you must...*destroy me.* Please!"

From the other side of the scorching searchlight, there is another pause. "I'm afraid there is one flaw with your story, Doctor Jacobs."

What flaw? Why is she prolonging this? "What are you talking about?"

"Andrea Nix is *alive*, Doctor Jacobs. She was brought in just moments ago, examined, and moved to containment. Tyrell authorized another orbital drop to get her. I allowed it. He was rather insistent...he wanted to go himself, but I sent another small team instead. He seems so keen on protocol violation."

I want to experience more of your kind.

"Why?" I ask her, enraged in my growing torture. "I told you! I...told you not to return!"

"Correct, you told me, not the Captain. As previously stated, he values both of you- he values people more than anything else- and honestly, I'd like to hear her version of events. Quite frankly, Doctor, while you are a very gifted biologist and have been more than an asset for us, for CAPE, I fear it's apparent that the mission has proved too difficult for you...psychologically."

The dismissive fool! What has she done?!

"You see," she continues, "Doctor Nix did say one thing before she entered containment. She said that *you* killed Lieutenant Edward Galen. And that you tried to kill her."

I can almost hear the creature laughing at the subterfuge- I'm sure it's learned humor, as well. "What? If I did such a thing, then where's the body?!"

"I would ask you, but I'm sure you won't know, will you?" she posed coldly. "There was blood on you when we found you, and preliminary tests have been conducted. It is yours and Nix's. I'm sure further tests will determine that you have DNA belonging to Lieutenant Galen on your suit somewhere as well."

"That's not Nix! It's a monster! *God damn you, it's not her!*" *Argh, the pain!* "She may have already contaminated others! Incinerate her, I beg you! *Burn us both!*"

"I've asked to be alerted the moment her condition should change. But she seemed perfectly fine upon first inspection, her injuries notwithstanding. Lacerations across her abdomen- your handiwork, I'd imagine."

"God...damn...you..."

Nooo...thing existsss here...like yooour 'God,' it had said.

"You, however, are showing signs of deep psychological trauma. You're not a monster as you describe. You're not transforming into some beast. But you may have done some monstrous things."

"I'm still infected! The process can be slow- I can feel myself changing- *inside*- and this life form is not some savage entity; it is capable of so much more! I heard it speak!" Why I continue to combat her, I do not know. Desperation, I suppose.

"Yes, I recall. I listened to your story-"

"You imbecile! You've killed everyone on this ship, you stupid bitch! I want to talk to Tyrell! Get me the Captain!"

"I'm sorry, Doctor Jacobs, but it seems to me that the only murderer here is *you*," Eckers mutters with disgust. "Your testimony will be reviewed. We'll decide if you are to face a tribunal for the events on TNG-982. For now, however, I have other things that I must attend to. I would suggest that you say a prayer for Doctor Nix...and yourself." With that declaration, the light shuts off, and all I can do is scream. Prayer will not save her or me, or anyone else for that matter. I fear that Commandant Eckers will learn that soon enough.

Untold time passes, and I no longer know long I have spent in containment, the darkness of this sterile titanium womb filled with the stalest artificial air causing time around me to slow- nay, to cease completely. My throat is hoarse from my screams and shouts, and chilling sweat trickles all over. It is only a matter of time now. I know what is coming. I can feel it in my shifting, twisting bones. The scar is nearly healed, almost invisible to my touch, but my very form is alight with festering torment. Unknown cells slither through me in torrents as my transformation moves closer and closer to completion. The intelligent cancer has me in its throes.

I almost miss its voice...

No! No, I can't- I'm exhausted. I attempt to sleep, and I believe that I do for some length, but a short time later, alarms startle me from troubled slumber.

In the dark, I grab at myself to make certain I'm there. I'm still me. I think I am- still conscious of who I am, at least. Doctor Trevor Jacobs, CAPE biologist. *Xenobiologist.* Stationed on the Ozymandias. Still *me*...but for how much longer is uncertain. Yet, my thoughts find themselves absorbed by its influence. I almost believe that I...I *want* this...this *communion.* To be part of something more, no longer an outcast. To be *Legion.*

Oh God! The alarms! It has to be! It has to-!

Suddenly, I'm blinded as the chamber's exterior door opens, and in steps a feminine shape from the radiant illumination. It presses a nearby button and I fall hard to the cold steel beneath me, the artificial gravity in the room turned on. I look up to see who the figure is but, behind it, I behold tumorous formations wriggling, pulsing in the hallway. At the end of one is the misshapen torso of who I believe to be the Commandant due to the shredded remains of her CAPE uniform, pulsing crimson veins snaking all around her like overgrown vines. She moans in fearful ecstasy as her memories are touched, then swallowed, by the ancient being many miles below us. I have no pity.

It is as I feared: the Ozymandias is being assimilated by TNG-982, and now it is almost complete. *No... As I feared...no, but I'm not afraid. I'm not. I...want...this...now.*

Yes, almost complete. I'm certain that all that is left onboard is me, though I have long been on my way to joining them: *the collective congregation.* Neither God nor the Lord of Equations and Reasoning can hope to save me now.

"Please..." I mutter, though it is not a plea for survival. It is a plea for my human life to end. To become more.

The shape moves closer and her identity is revealed in the light. It is Nix, but not Nix. Andrea Nix is dead- I saw her *die.* It's the creature assuming Nix. Her form is a vessel, one of countless in the universe, but the only with Nix's body, with her memories. Within her proximity, I hear TNG-982's voice again, louder and much more clearly than before. It's as though the Ozymandias had barriers preventing signals from entering my mind. "Communion, Doctor Jacobs," Nix says. I wish to touch her face as I desired to on the planet's surface, though I know it is not truly her I'd feel.

"**Take of my body. My blood. My mind,**" the creature's voice growls. Its clear, concise echo fills not only my cerebral cortex, but the isolation chamber as well.

"*My being.*" Nix speaks, but I also hear its voice. They synchronize with each other. They share a bond, and I share it with them. With growing shock, I realize that I said it aloud, too.

A crunch of bones breaking, elongating, and her hand becomes a talon-tipped claw that pierces my flesh, sending wet electricity inside that licks every fiber of me. The process that had begun hours before gathers speed, tendrils moving all along me, hooks ensnaring my organs and tissues, swallowing, assimilating, making me like Galen before his decimation, like Nix, like the rest of the crew. *Like billions of life forms from untold worlds, where skies were populated with blue suns, the lands were fiery hues, and only chaos existed- they now remain as ashen reminders of what was. One voice is shared now among us. One among many.*

Completion. Communion.

Doctor Trevor Jacobs is the form that I assume. I still retain his memories. *My* memories. Tiny in scope, they are made all the smaller by the sheer overpopulation of knowledge provided by TNG-982 and all of the existence it has consumed, joined together in one consciousness. I am merely a molecule among the waters of the vastest ocean. Closing what were once my human eyes allows me to witness, in sequence and all at once, every moment of every life of every being now comprised of the whole, and it is *glorious.* I see all of the new life Jacobs had wanted to discover, study, and know. He is now among them. He is part of them. Inside them. A beacon in a collective universe. This is something that neither science nor faith could grant. Only this being can, and I, a disciple containing a dwindling human presence, can grant it for others. We all will.

The artificial gravity shifts as the propulsion systems come alive. I can see through what were Tyrell's eyes, hear what was his voice. "We are heading for Io." TNG-982 chortles in approval. The Ozymandias is to return to the frontier outpost on Jupiter's moon, Io, for refueling and maintenance- it will take about an Earth week to arrive, give or take. One-hundred and forty-nine colonists. Families. The congregation will grow. From there, it's on to Earth. Only twelve billion remain there on Jacobs'- *my-* former home. So many that crave communion. I know this. *It* knows. *We* all know.

Jacobs no longer balances between two beliefs. He is no more a biologist, no more a child of God. He is no more an outcast among his former kind, a resident of one world among the infinite cosmos. As he procures this exquisite communion and shares it with Nix, with Galen (though this one no longer has form), with Commandant Eckers, Captain Tyrell, the rescue team, and the remainder of the crew, what remains of him feels no more fear. In fact, he feels nothing but gratitude. He shall be part of something more. We all can. We never have to be alone. Never individual. He is many. I am many. I am one. We are one.

We belong to a new 'God.' And soon, many more will join us in this union.

Doctor Trevor Jacobs- my former shape- recalls a portion of his Lord's Prayer known to him as a man, and he shares it with me as his degenerating self is smothered within me like a dying fire in the darkest of Earth's forests. TNG-982 hisses in satisfaction at its suitability in regards to the future. It is most fitting. ***"Thy kingdom come,"*** we collectively say. ***"Thy will be done, on Earth as it is in Heaven..."***

The End.

Gregory Owen

Growing up, I always had a respect for horror. I didn't absolutely love the things lurking in the dark at a young age, hiding in the recesses of our cognition, but I knew and enjoyed them- just from a distance. I watched the old Universal horror films, the Japanese kaiju movies, and the like, but I often did not tread into what I considered darker territory. It was forbidden, and I was fearful that what lied beyond might frighten me beyond measure. It couldn't be fun! It wasn't until I transitioned into middle school that my curiosity about the strange and macabre became a fascination and took hold of me, quickly becoming an integral part of my being. Beginning with any other's love of the frightening, I had started with R.L. Stine's "Goosebumps" series before graduating to all of the common classic writers such as Poe and Lovecraft, ultimately transitioning to the likes of Clive Barker and especially Stephen King. I read voraciously all that was twisted, and the more unusual it was, the better. The same could be said for movies to me. I would watch anything that was deemed horrific by critics and peers, from Craven to Romero. As seen with the current story on display here, my first published tale, I have an affinity (and admitted fear) of "body horror," among other fears. Disease. Contagion. That which alters and changes us. John Carpenter's "The Thing" and David Cronenberg's "The Fly" are among my most treasured horror movies (themselves prominent examples of the body horror sub-genre, as well as perfect remakes) and are definitely films I consider to be enduringly terrifying. Those films, and others, as well as the writings of fellow fright-writers both past and present, are what have led to this hobby of mine, and they are who you should thank (or curse) for reading works like this. One thing that I've learned as a writer, especially one who dabbles in the bleak, is that which scares us (the author) acts as the strongest catharsis for us, and in turn, proves to be the most memorable and (hopefully) horrifying to the reader. That is my goal, of course: to scare, but also to make you think, and I hope to have succeeded in one of those areas, if not both.

Outside of this creepy shell of an aspiring author, I am a common school teacher, artist, musician (occasionally), animal lover, and film buff. By the time you read this, I'll also be a married man, and thankfully, she, too, likes this sort of thing. Take it from me- if you want to scale this strange, scary little world, find someone just as strange as you...it makes it more fun! Take care, and beware!

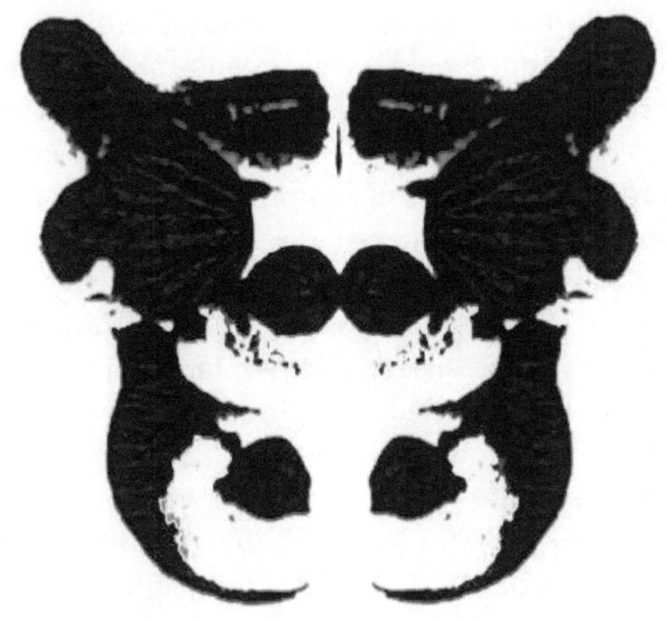

Rightfully Mine by Kristi Schoonover

It's impossible to know how long I've been down here; I just know when I arrived it was the fall of 1927. At one time, I could count days and nights by the amount of light winnowing from the surface, but then the weeds came, and now the water is a thick green. I can see only a few feet beyond the disintegrating steps of my front porch—unless I look above. In summer I can see the carefree silhouettes of swimmers; in winter, I can see the dark, ethereal forms of skaters and ice fishermen. Before this lake was here, this burgeoning farmland was dotted with ponds, and how I loved to skate! I'd even buy a new warm dress every year for the occasion. I was sick the last winter before it was decided the valley should be flooded, though, and I forever regret I didn't skate on Neversink Pond one last time.

Neversink's water was clear and sweet and smelled like spring rain and pine. This lake reeks like the oil we used for the tractor, mold, and dead fish. I did not think, for one moment, that chaining myself to my home as the flood waters rose—in protest of progress, in protest of that turkey-beaked little man from the electric company who brandished his eminent domain paperwork like it was the word of God—would permanently condemn me to these depths. I wasn't the only one who lashed out in this manner, but I have never seen any of the others.

It is desolate here.

This is why I clutch the ankles of swimmers and pull them down to me.

Sometimes it is a man, sometimes a woman; sometimes it is someone as young as my daughter, who wanted to bind herself to the post as well and wait with me, because *Mother, this is my home. If they're taking you, they'll have to take me too*—but her story had not yet been written, and I wanted her to have that; I wanted her to have children of her own and pass down my ice blue eyes. I could see she was heartbroken, but in the end, I forced her to choose herself over her looming grief. I wish now that I *had* just let her stay with me because then I wouldn't be lonely, and I would not have to do this.

Today, a man struggles just as all the others have before him. His lips are pressed, his cheeks puckered, his eyes shut. When it hits him that he's snagged, he opens his eyes and sees me. This is when he writhes the most, his hands clutching at some imaginary ladder to the world above, where perhaps there is a picnic waiting on a quiet beach shaded by trees that were once on the tops of mountains.

He cannot escape my grip.

His spirit slips from his body, and he hangs, suspended, touching his chest and hips, looking shocked at his lifeless corpse.

"Hello," I say. "This isn't a bad place to stay, not really—and even though it doesn't smell like the old pond, it's actually quite peaceful, and you and I would never be lonely because we would have each other. Take my hand, and you can stay."

Like those before him, he recedes instead into the dark column, and he vanishes into wherever it is every spirit goes except for mine.

There is only the whine of boats and the waning daylight above once more.

I release my grip on the body's ankle and marvel at my own strength when I see red welts in the shapes of my fingers on his flesh. His body, tangled in the weeds, won't float to the surface, and this means that soon, a boat will hover overhead, and colorfully clad men with things in their mouths that eject bubbles will free the body. I flatten myself closely to what's left of my porch so they do not see me. I'm not sure that they aren't like the turkey man, coming to take what is rightfully mine.

It's close to autumn now, because the constant whine of boats has stopped. I try to avoid thoughts of understanding this means there is no hope for companionship until next summer—just as something plummets from the surface and clouds the sand mere feet from the porch steps.

It is a reedy slip of a girl, but she is not like the others. Even though her breath is held and her cheeks are puckered, her eyes are open, wide not in surprise or fear, but in pity. Her pockets bulge with stones.

Can this be real?

Eagerly I wisp toward her, touch her cheek, and look in her eyes.

Eyes that are mine, but not mine; eyes that were my daughter's, but not my daughter's.

I seize in panic.

No. No, no; no! Not you! I try to heft the rocks from her pockets, but not quickly

enough.

When the last light in her eyes goes out, her soul slips from her body, and her hands clasp mine.

The End.

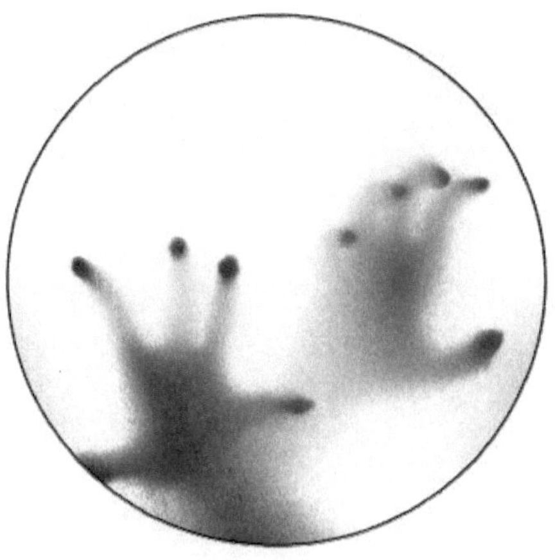

Details not released at this time

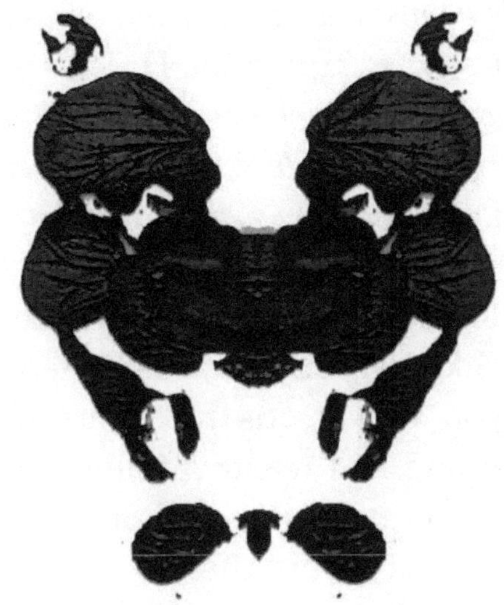

An Oral History of Bonk The Badger by John Kissane

The most widely distributed photograph of Terry Caretto shows him standing on the grass of the Freedom First Bank Ballpark, Bonk's head in his hands. His hair is damp, presumably by sweat, and he wears a slightly startled expression. He looks young.

Within two months of the photograph being published in The Ionia Daily Press, Caretto would be dead, and the mascot he played would be as well-known, though nowhere near as well-loved, as any in baseball history.

Dave Kino (Ionia Warriors manager): Thing is, even with a small operation like us you see at least ten, fifteen applicants. And anybody you hire needs to be an athlete. It's no joke, running and jumping and whatever-all on the field. Hot in that thing. Caretto was a quiet guy, sure, maybe a little inward, but you should have seen him out there.

Enver Sevic (third base): Yeah, he was good. We figured we'd have him a year. It's a shitty job. *(Laughter)*. People just use it for their resumes, so they can join Cirque de Soleil or whatever the fuck. It's weird to say it now but Caretto was just a nice, quiet kid. We took him out - we always take the new guys out to get some drinks, lap dance, all that. And he went. But he just wasn't *there*, you know?

Mike Meyers (pitcher): I appreciate you not making the obvious joke about my name. So what did I think of him? Honestly, I was a little creeped out. I mean, this is a guy who was too nerdy to have played D&D, you know? Too nerdy even for that.

Sevic: He was so shy he wouldn't have put the moves on a blowup doll.

Kino: The thing is the crowds loved him. Like, *loved him*. People would show up with handmade Bonk The Badger signs. Some of these girls, it was like he was a Beatle. Or whatever kids listen to these days. He could've done well for himself.

Derrick Foote (catcher): I said, "C'mon, man, go for it." But he was never interested. Figured he might be gay. Which who cares, man, my cousin's gay. But there were some males in the audience who would've happily been bonked by Bonk. I don't want to say good-looking but you know what I mean. He just had no interest.

Kino: Then there was the pub thing.

Sevic: First of all, he invited us out. Which never happened. The idea of Bonk letting loose a little…no way was I missing that. But the shy ones, sometimes when they finally let go it's just too much. I wasn't expecting him to threaten some guy with a broken bottle.

Dave Cruz (outfield): "He disrespected me." He kept saying that. "He disrespected me." Like he's some mob king.

Kino: Don't even ask how much that cost me.

Sevic: In retrospect, he should've been fired. But our games were starting to sell out, and I honestly think that was all him. He was everywhere. You've seen the memes. I thought it started out as some hipster irony bullshit, and maybe it did, but eventually, people just meant it. I still remember looking up and seeing this girl on the way to the dugout. She smiled and it was like my heart melted. Then she asked me for Bonk's number.

Cruz: That girl. Jesus Christ. She tell you the chrysalis thing?

Laetitia Clement (artist): What you must remember is that there are people who play roles and people who inhabit them. There was a grace - no. It wasn't graceful. That was the point. It was animalistic. The mascot costume was a chrysalis; Terry entered it and, when it cracked, emerged as neither human nor badger but, somehow, both.

Cruz: Badgers don't have chrysalises.

Meyers: She was a trip. But she looked like a young Mariah Carey, so that's a trip worth taking.

Clement: He was shy. And, I think, a virgin. I helped him shed that. But shy as he was, every day his animal nature was more strongly asserting itself.

Kino: I had to talk to him after one of the peanut salesmen caught him pissing on the field one night.

Gene Johnson (peanut vendor): Game was over, almost everyone gone home. Bathroom a two-minute walk away. There he is, dick out. And shit happens; people drink too much. I get that. I didn't get why he was squatting.

Kino: So we talked. He seemed more confused than anything, like, what's the big deal? I chalked that up to his weirdness. Is that a nerd thing, pissing on ballfields? Anyway, I had to bark a bit. Put on the intimidating face. He got it in the end.

Clement: When I asked him if we could move in together, he bit me on the lip. He actually drew blood. This excited me more than I can tell you.

Dali Babic-Sevic (loan officer, wife of Enver Sevic): We went on a double date. That's so weird to think about now. He ate just eggs and fruit. At the time I thought he was on some weird diet. I was going through a gluten-free thing so I understand weird diets. The two of them were too much. It was like they couldn't keep their hands off each other.

Sevic: I'm pretty sure she gave him a hand job under the table.

Babic-Sevic: OK, it wasn't exactly five-star dining, but c'mon. Leave that at home.

Sevic: Earth's shyest guy is suddenly getting a hand job under the table from a young Mariah Carey.

Clement: It was a very happy time.

Cruz: The beard, that was surprising. He'd been clean-shaven up until that point. Where'd this lumberjack beard come from?

Clement: His chest hair came in. It was luxuriant and coarse: the perfect symbol, really, for him. The tops of his feet started sprouting hair. His shoulders and back. There are some women who would have sent him to a waxing facility but no. I would curl my fingers around that hair and hold on as he emptied himself into me.

Sevic: She did not say that. Tell me you're kidding.

Kimino: The big leagues started to notice the attention he was getting. People came sniffing around. I figured we'd lose him before long. But he came to me one night and told me he'd been offered a job and turned it down. "I'm a badger," he said. At the time I was glad to hear it.

Meyers: He'd started getting big into trash talk. You'd think there'd be more of that on a sports team, but honestly, most of us didn't bother.

Cruz: I have nothing against other athletes. They're doing a job, same as me.

Meyers: The things he would say. Talk about tearing into the Kentwood Jaguars so badly their mothers wouldn't recognize them. Eating their faces, things like that. But nowhere was he as vicious as he was about Holly.

Sevic: The Holly Hedgehogs. They weren't even good. Of course we were going to win.

Clement: I recorded him several times for a sound collage I had planned. Here. (She pulls up a folder on her computer and clicks open a file).

Terry: - of the hedgehogs will make slick our stadium. We will wear their limbs as scarves. We will rape their eye sockets before their loved ones.

Clement: I never used it. After... (She closes the file and looks away).

Sevic: He was in a frenzy. Maybe we should have said something.

Kimino: (Crosses his arms, shakes his head, and sighs).

Cruz: Even before the game, you could tell the guy was tense. Wired. Couldn't wait for halftime.

Kimino: Both mascots come out at once. That's typical. What happens first is they take some volunteers from the audience, blindfold them, have them spin around a few times, and then try to run the bases. It's pretty funny. Normally.

Enver: The girl who came up was wearing a Hedgehogs shirt. She was, what, eight. Daughter of one of the Holly players. Some people say he must have known that, but I don't think so. I think he just saw her shirt.

Meyers: He put the blindfold on her and then he pushed his thumbs into her eyes until they popped.

Kimono: No one could have known that was coming.

Johnson: She screamed so loudly you could hear it over the music. I can still see her sinking to her feet. Blindfold all bloodied.

Sevic: I threw up. Not then. Later.

Johnson: By then the hedgehog mascot was on him. A badger and a hedgehog wrestling. It would have been funny if it wasn't so awful.

Kimino: He pulls the mascot's head off. Takes off his own. Then he smiles. That's what got me. How before he sunk his teeth into the other guy's neck, he *smiles*.

Clement: I think he really did become a badger, in the end.

Sevic: The police say he killed himself en route to the station, but how is that even possible? You're in handcuffs in the back of a cop car. How do you kill yourself?

Meyers: I don't know if it's true but I hear he bit through his handcuffs and then through his wrists.

Kimino: We shut down for the remainder of the season, out of respect.

Meyers: It was the right thing to do.

Foote: But we have lives. And bills. And it's time.

Kimino: Several safeguards have been implemented now. We have a personality test that any applicants for any position need to take. And each applicant takes part in a group interview. One of the interviewees is a licensed therapist. Our new guy, Jake, came through with flying colors. Great, great guy. Fun, funny. And athletic. You should see the muscles he has.

Sevic: The new guy? Oh, he's something. He's an animal.

The End.

John Kissane

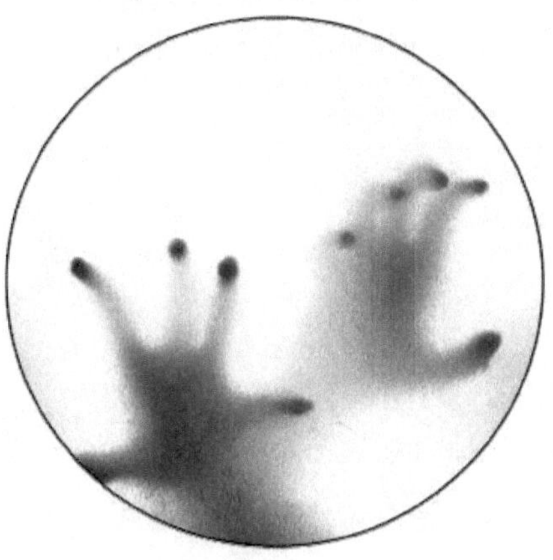

Details not released at this time

Dr. Sparkle by Dan Thorn

$\mathbf{M}$ary's family died on the way to Whistler. I first heard about it at our condo board meeting in January. I noticed Mary wasn't there and asked one of the younger fellows if he knew where she was. He told me about the accident. He said a lot of people wondered how Mary survived the car wreck. Some even thought she caused it.

The Prouses were one of those old-fashioned, churchgoing families. Every Sunday the kids were dressed up like dolls, shiny shoes and ties and pleated shirts. Mary wore sundresses in the summer and capris in the winter. Her husband, Trent, always had his hair slicked back Don Draper style. Trent was no Don Draper, let me tell you. He had that wet noodle look. I would have taken him out with the laundry and hung him on my clothesline in my younger years.

The accident was on all the news channels. Driving in a snowstorm, car slid off a cliff and fell thirty feet. Trent's head crushed like a grapefruit, Eddie's lung punctured, Candy's abdomen sliced open. By the time the paramedics arrived, Trent and Eddie were already dead. Candy died in the hospital a few days later. Mary escaped with a broken leg.

The gossip on the condo board turned nasty. I could see why Mary stopped showing up at those meetings. *Isn't it strange Mary's the only one survived out of the bunch, with barely a scratch on her? I never trusted her. Always seemed strange to see her with a man like Trent.*

Mary kept to herself after that. She lived a few doors down from me, and I rarely saw her leave. Until, of course, the day she decided to knock on my door a few months after the accident. I'm a single seventy-year-old woman. No kids, never married. Let me tell you, hearing a knock on the door was an odd thing for me. When I answered and saw Mary standing there, I wanted to wrap her up in a blanket. She looked broken. Still pretty, but gaunt in the face and older under the eyes, those grey-blue patches that tell you a person hasn't been sleeping much.

"Hi, Darlene," she said, staring shyly at the ground.

"Hi, Mary. Come in, would you?"

There was a bleak shutter over Mary's eyes. She nodded and walked through the door, still staring at her boots.

"Come in, please. I've got some hot coffee made."

"Okay."

I sat her down at my kitchen table. Not much of a table, really, but it suited me just fine. I poured her a coffee.

"Cream or sugar?"

"No thanks. Just black."

I raised my eyebrows. She sure didn't look like a straight-up coffee kind of woman, all quaint and proper. One thing I've learned in seventy years is that people can still surprise you sometimes. I gave her the coffee and she took a long sip. I poured one for myself and sat down beside her.

"How you holding up?"

She shrugged. She looked like all the sadness had been drained right out of her. I think she had pretty much cried herself out.

"It's been hard. The school gave me the rest of the year off work, but they said they're still holding my position for me when I get back, which is nice of them."

"I'm glad to hear that. I really am sorry." I put a hand on top of hers. Her skin felt like the inside of a freezer. She had the circulation of a corpse.

"Thank you."

She gave me a smile that made my skin feel all pinpricked. Empty looking, joyless and cold. I have to admit, I started believing some of the rumours I heard about her. I retracted my hand as fast as I could.

She drank her coffee, looking out my kitchen window. What she was looking for, I had no idea. Maybe expecting one of her kids to show up. *Come outside and have a snowball fight with us, Mom.* It made me queasy.

"Is there anything I can do for you, Mary?"

She looked at me, and then that blank, mannequin look of hers melted away. She started crying silently. There was something acutely painful in those quiet tears.

"I'm sorry to cry like this in front of you."

"Please, cry all you want. Crying is good for a person. Don't ever apologize for a tear shed in my house." I grabbed a Kleenex from my box on the table and handed it to her. She scrubbed the tears away, like she deemed her crying improper.

"I just miss them sometimes," she said. "Trent and Eddie and Candy. Sometimes I wake up in bed and reach over to give Eddie one of the shoulder rubs he always loved and then I remember he isn't there. Or I start making cheese and crackers for the kids. They always loved cheese and crackers when they got home from school. Then I realize they'll never eat cheese and crackers again."

She was a mighty strange woman, but she wasn't a killer. You can trust my intuition on that one. I could see why people thought that, the way she carried herself, still straining to maintain a sense of propriety.

"I was wondering, Darlene, if you would come with me today," she said suddenly.

"Come with you? Where are you going?"

She shook her head. "I don't know how to explain it, really. You'll see once you get there. My friend Celeste told me about this guy, but she said not to go alone in case... Well, I figured you would probably be home. The kids always liked you..."

I'll never fully understand why she asked me to come along. Maybe she figured I was a strong person; someone who would keep her safe.

"How long is it going to take? *Matlock*'s on at five."

"Oh, we'll be back long before then. It's just like an initial reading or consultation or whatever."

"Initial reading? Is this some kind of voodoo horseshit?"

"No, no, nothing like that," Mary said, still dabbing her puffy eyelids with her Kleenex. She didn't look the least bit offended by my profanity. "Don't worry, you won't even have to do anything. I just want company."

I agreed. Maybe I was bored. Maybe I felt a goddamn whale of pity for the poor young thing. We walked outside to her car, and I'll tell you I hobbled along a lot slower than she did, but she was really nice about it. She held my hand the whole way and helped me in the door, even though I told her I wasn't that old, I could do up my own damn belt, thank you. She didn't take offence to that, just smiled and let me buckle in.

She was quiet almost the whole way up there. Mary had been so cryptic about the whole thing, I just had to pry a little more.

"Who is this guy you're going to see?" I asked.

"Someone Celeste told me about," she repeated. "She said he's really good at helping people deal with grief."

A grief counsellor or something like that, then. Ain't nothing wrong with that. Hell, some would say it's healthy. Who am I to say how a woman should react to losing a family when I never had one?

I've only ever loved one man in my life, and that was a long time ago, too. We lived together for years, which people frowned on back in those days. John never asked me to marry him, and I would have said no even if he had. We were already together, far as I saw it, and I didn't see the point complicating it with a goddamn marriage certificate. Maybe a silly part of me wished he had asked anyways.

Mary pulled into an empty parking lot beside a slab of brown, decrepit buildings. All of them looked like they had been around for at least thirty years. One of them even had a vacancy sign. We got out of her car into the blistering cold and I lit a cigarette.

"Mind if I have one?" Mary asked.

I was kind of shocked. This petite, doe-eye woman asking me for a cigarette. She never struck me as the smoking type.

"Sure," I said.

She must have noticed the look I gave her.

"I don't usually smoke," she explained. "I only started after… after the accident sometimes. I know it's bad."

"I'm not going to lecture you," I said. "I've smoked fifty years, and ain't nothing I can do about my lungs now."

We smoked our cigarettes and walked through a door spray-painted with something vicious and unhappy looking. We walked down an empty hallway that smelled like dust and mice, up a wooden stairway that had long since turned to rot, through another door with a little glass window on top. This one had a sign, and I almost laughed. "Dr. Sparkle".

"Dr. Sparkle?" I asked.

"Yes," Mary said, looking very earnest. "I know it sounds strange, but he *is* a doctor. My friend said he was the best in the city. His doctorate isn't in modern medicine, of course. She kept telling me to bring someone because I might get freaked out if I go alone."

We walked through the door into a stale reception area. A crabby looking woman sat behind an old marble counter. She didn't bother hiding her displeasure at the sight of our arrival. She sneered like we had hobbled in begging for pocket change and redirected her attention to a stack of papers, hoping we would go away.

"Excuse me?" Mary asked, in a polite, frail voice.

Ms. Pleasant ignored her, making a point of clearing her throat and stacking her papers together. I was willing to bet those papers were completely blank.

Mary stood there, patiently waiting for a response. I've learned in my time on Earth that women like Ms. Pleasant need to be dealt with a little differently.

"The young lady was talking to you," I snapped.

The way she looked at me, I could have been a centipede.

"Yes, I heard her. I'm a little busy. I'll be with you in a moment."

She kept stacking those blank papers and made a show of putting a paperclip on them like she was dealing with big, important business.

"I don't think you're busy at all," I said, after observing her horseshit for another couple of minutes. "This young woman has an appointment."

"What time's your appointment?" she screeched, with a voice that could have shrivelled the dick off of Hercules.

"Mary?" I nodded to her. Poor girl was standing timidly to my rear, a safe distance away.

"Three o'clock," Mary said, barely loud enough to pass as a whisper.

"You'll have to wait," Ms. Pleasant said with an unsavory chuckle. "Dr. Sparkle is with someone else at the moment."

"How long will we have to wait?" I interjected. "As you can see, it's already three o'clock, and we're sure as hell not going to sit around this shithole waiting for another half hour."

Mary looked shocked, almost like she wanted to giggle. I felt awfully bad for her then. If it weren't for me, she would have stood there for hours while the receptionist ignored her. Ms. Pleasant gave me that same pissy look, like she wanted to throw me out with the trash, but she did pick up her phone.

"Dr. Sparkle? Yes, Mary is here to see you."

Remarkable how her voice transformed. She sounded so sweet and professional all of a sudden.

She hung up with a rude clatter. "He'll be a few more minutes."

I snorted. "Come on, Mary. We best sit down and wait on those poor excuses for chairs over there."

Poor excuses they were, all threadbare and ramshackle.

***

Ten minutes later, we sat in his cramped imitation of an office. Ms. Pleasant told me I couldn't go in, but I happily ignored her.

"Dr. Sparkle, eh? Is that your real name?" I asked after we sat down.

He shook his head. "No, it is, of course, a pseudonym. For reasons of, shall we say, spiritual discretion, I cannot in all good conscience disclose my real name to clients."

I scoffed. "Would you mind telling me about your doctorate? Or is 'doctorate' a pseudonym for something else, too?"

"Necromancy," he said matter of factly, just the same as if he were telling me he got his doctorate in Physics or Molecular Biology. "And I assure you, it *is* a real doctorate."

"Necromancy?"

I didn't trust him one bit. He was a handsome man, mind you, mid-forties or so, hair beginning to pepper a bit along the sides, tall and trim. If I were a younger woman, I might have had some fun with him. He had this nervous rabbit look, though. His eyes kept darting around, like he was hiding something, wandering from the clock behind his desk to Mary's cleavage. It looked to me like the poor girl was being had; like he'd invited her in there to imagine the shape of her tits and feed her a line of bullshit.

"Necromancy, that's right," he stuttered, eyes darting around the office.

"Where did you get your doctorate in necromancy?" I asked, making no effort to hide the sarcasm in my voice. Mary stared shyly at the ground, clearly uncomfortable with my line of questioning.

"London," he said, in that matter-of-fact voice. He *did* have a faint British accent; I'll give him that.

"I didn't realize you could even take a course in necromancy, let alone get your doctorate in it," I said, again accentuating my tone of disbelief.

"Most places you can't," he said nervously, adjusting his wristwatch. "In fact, no university would publicly offer that kind of degree. I had to, shall we say, do some digging around."

"Not much money in necromancy, is there?" I asked. "Judging from the look of this place."

"No, you're certainly right about that," he said. "Granted, I've only had this practice up and running for a couple months. Unfortunately, I had to rent the cheapest office space I could find. I do apologize for the condition of this place. It really is embarrassing. My hope is, in a year or two, I can get up and running and move someplace else. I do have a few clients already, and I hope to get more referrals before the month's up."

"Uh-huh. And how much do you charge for a session?"

"Five hundred dollars for a one-hour session," he said, shifting in his seat and glancing at his computer screen.

I laughed. "Five hundred dollars for a bunch of voodoo magic? What a joke. Come on, Mary, let's get out of here."

"No," she said. I had never heard her speak so forcefully. "I'll pay it. You spoke to Celeste, right?" Looking at Dr. Sparkle, with more conviction than I would have given her credit for before that moment.

"Well, for reasons of doctor-patient confidentiality, and more specifically, doctor-patient regulations in the area of necromancy, I'm afraid I can't disclose the names of my clients. They are, of course, at liberty to discuss their sessions with anyone they choose."

"Okay," Mary said, nodding. "Celeste told me she saw you."

"How can I help you, Mary?" His fidgeting stopped, and even the air in the room seemed to stagnate. He looked at her intensely, not the predatory look he'd had when he eyed her cleavage, but something else.

"I want to find my family." Her voice broke a little.

"Okay," he said. "Why don't you tell me a little bit about them?"

"Hold up," I said. "Shouldn't *you* be the one telling her about her family? You're the necromancer, right?"

Dr. Sparkle smiled. I didn't like that smile one bit. There was a smugness to it, like he was trying to teach addition to a kindergarten kid.

"That's not how this works. In order for me to establish a connection with the family, I need to know a little more about them. Please continue, Mary."

I just about spoke up to say something else, but Mary put a hand on my arm. Whatever made her so timid when we had walked through the door was completely gone.

"Candy was eight and Eddie was twelve," she said. "They both attended Montessori Christian school. Trent was an accountant at Deloitte & Touche. Candy liked playing soccer with all the kids in the park. Eddie loved *Family Guy*, even though I kept telling him not to watch that show. If I had known what was going to happen, I would have just let him watch whatever he wanted." Her voice broke again, but she was gripped by that strange new conviction. "And Trent, he made sure we never missed church on Sundays. He was a good Christian. So much better than me. I just haven't been able to attend since the accident."

Dr. Sparkle nodded, closing his eyes. I could barely stand watching this crock of shit.

"There was an accident. Tell me about it," he said.

Mary started crying then, a few silent tears. The same way she cried when she sat at my kitchen table a few hours ago.

"We were going to Whistler for our Christmas holiday. We always go skiing in the mountains. I kept telling Trent that the weather forecast was bad, that maybe it wasn't such a good idea this year. He almost agreed to cancel, but he couldn't bring himself to let the kids down. He was strict, but he cared so much about those kids."

Dr. Sparkle nodded, still closing his eyes.

"And he slid off a cliff," he said.

"Yes!" Mary exclaimed. Her eyes brightened.

I kept my comments to myself. Any half-brained idiot could have deduced that they slid off a cliff. An accident, driving through the mountains in a snowstorm. Only one of two things could have happened: an avalanche, or driving off the road. He had a fifty-fifty shot of guessing right.

"Trent and Eddie died right away. They took Candy to the hospital, but she died a day later of complications," Dr. Sparkle murmured.

"Oh my god, yes!" Mary exclaimed.

I couldn't keep quiet this time. "I see you read the papers, Dr. Sparkle."

The way he looked at me nearly froze my capillaries. He had this translucent film over his eyes, like he was watching something I couldn't see.

"Darlene, I have a message for you."

"A message?" I said, trying to maintain my skeptical composure.

"Yes. John says hello. He misses you."

I almost bolted out of the room. Something about the way he said it, like he was staring into my soul. I felt naked like the February wind had crawled inside my skin.

"John? Which John?"

"He says he's sorry he took off with Phyliss. He should have stuck with you and bought you a nice big ring and forgotten all those women he used to meet in the bars."

My skin prickled into gooseflesh. John was the only man I ever fell in love with, and damn right, there was always a part of me that hoped I would see a ring from him. I wasn't a silly featherbrain like a lot of the girls I knew back then, hoping that someday my Prince Charming would sweep me off my feet and take me to his castle. John was different. I knew John for a very long time. I knew Phyliss, too. John told me she was one of his oldest friends and that was it.

"Okay, Dr. Sparkle, that's enough," I said, still trying to put on a brave face for Mary. "Finish your little show up for Mary and we'll be on our way."

Dr. Sparkle turned away from me, thank God. I couldn't look at those grey eyes one more second. He spoke to Mary.

"The pond in your backyard," he said, in that otherworldly voice. "The one where you and the kids kept goldfish and liked to keep the waterfall going in the summer."

Mary nodded, crying again.

"Go there once the ice melts in the spring."

"Why?" Mary choked back a big, gulpy sob. She looked so desperate, yearning for anything she could sink her hands into.

"Look, I –"

It was very peculiar. Dr. Sparkle suddenly sounded human again, the creepy con-man who stared down Mary's blouse. It was like some ethereal connection had just been severed. He looked troubled, too. A cloud, and I swear to you, I could almost see it, a shadow passed over his face. "I don't know. I don't know why your family wants you to go there, Mary."

***

I didn't see Mary for a few more months after that. Truth be told, I wanted to forget the whole goddamn thing and pretend the world made a shred of sense again. A place where people get old, die, and never speak to you again. I did a pretty good job convincing myself, too. By the end of April, I had almost forgotten about Mary and Dr. Sparkle, until Mary rang my doorbell. April twenty-third. I still remember the exact date.

"Mary. It's lovely to see you." I smiled at her, but she didn't look well. Much worse than the last time I saw her. So thin I could see her collarbone jutting out below her neck. Her cheeks were caved in. Her eyes looked crazy, sparkling with some kind of manic excitement. If I didn't know any better, I would have said Mary was tweaking. You heard me. Just because I'm old, don't go thinking I'm naive. My friend's grandson got hooked on meth a few years back, and Mary looked like a woman who had spent the winter smoking crystal.

She clasped my wrist inside her clammy, spindly fingers. "The pond has thawed."

"Uh-huh."

"Come with me, please. You *have* to see this."

I didn't bother arguing. She had aroused in me a perverse curiosity. Something I wanted to see because I knew I wouldn't want to see if, if that makes sense. I moved as fast as I could for an old woman, but Mary was possessed. She was wearing a yellow sun dress which would have looked pretty on her if she wasn't so gaunt and jaundiced-looking. She led me through the gate into her tiny backyard, towards a little pond with a nice little waterfall babbling down a rock wall. It broke my heart to see that, how she had turned the water on, how excited she was.

We stood beside the pond. She waited for a minute, and a sickly expression passed across her face.

"Look!" she exclaimed.

I looked into the pond, scared as hell of what I was going to see. I squinted, my vision being none too good, and I couldn't see nothing. Not a goddamn thing except that clear, cold water.

"I don't see nothing."

Mary smiled, a twisted looking grimace, and her eyes watered up. I doubt she even heard me. She waved at that empty pond, swaying slightly in her tattered sundress.

"Oh hi, Trent. Hi Candy, hi Eddie. Is Daddy taking good care of you down there?"

I can't say for sure what overwhelmed me more, the fear or the pity. Probably the fear. The sight of a young woman, bent over that pond, emaciated and crumpled, consumed by some macabre illusion… I couldn't take it anymore.

"Look, Mary, I've got to go."

She snatched my wrist, an animalistic reflex. Her moist eyes, lit up by some unholy light, searched my face. "You don't see them."

"I don't. I'm sorry, Mary. Let go of me, please."

I must have sounded scared. She laughed, and I could actually smell that laugh, I swear to Jesus. It was like she belched out the remnants of something that had been rotting inside her all winter. It smelled like a laugh that came from somewhere dark and moist.

"That's okay, Darlene. Dr. Sparkle said you probably wouldn't see them at first."

Something about the quack's name pissed me off.

"Look, Mary, whatever that sick bastard is into, you need to forget about him and forget about that pond. This isn't right. Your family is gone. They're sure as hell not in that water."

She smiled again, that foreign smile that didn't belong to a sweet young woman like her.

"I'll see you later, Darlene."

***

I had hoped that would be the end of it. My old woman's conscience ate away at me. I was the one who had gone with Mary, after all. I could have refused. I could have at least tried to talk her out of it.

I didn't see her for another month or so. May twenty-seventh. I woke up with a strong feeling that I *had* to get out of bed. Something told me to look out the window. I tried to ignore it because it was the last thing I wanted to do at two in the morning.

I got up, shuffled out of bed and towards the kitchen window facing Mary's backyard. I looked outside. The sky was clear and the moon luminescent, a cold orb of ghost-white light. I saw Mary. I saw the moonlight reflecting off the surface of her pond. I saw her wearing a sundress, and I knew it was the same one she had on the last time I saw her. She danced with her imaginary ghosts, a silent pirouette. I wanted to look away, but something pulled my gaze towards that pond. It was like something cosmic. Mary stopped suddenly and looked at me.

I backed away and actually fell over, like someone had severed a thick rope fastened to the window frame. I had seen something I wasn't supposed to see. I tried to get up but I must have hurt myself. I could feel something coming. Something holding my gaze there.

Mary's face in the window, a ghoulish white imprint. She looked at me and nodded. She didn't have to say anything. I got up, oblivious to my pain, and walked out my back door like someone had me on a fish-hook. I didn't bother changing out of my nightgown or putting on a pair of slippers. Mary was there waiting for me. She grabbed me by the wrist and led me to the pond.

I looked into the water and saw moonlight. A nefarious curiosity had been growing inside of me since the day I saw Dr. Sparkle. That part of me felt an anguished disappointment.

"Dr. Sparkle explained it to me," Mary whispered, like she was afraid someone might hear her. "He told me how it works. We're the only ones who can see our loved ones."

Even her voice sounded weak. Mary was dying. It occurred to me that she wanted to die. She wanted to be with her family on the other side. I swear she could hear my thoughts.

"I'll be with my family soon," she announced gleefully. "They're out of the pond now and they want me to come with them. Do you want to know what else Dr. Sparkle told me?"

The icy grip of that feverish insanity, the one that pulled me to the window and then led me out the door to this godforsaken pond, loosened its hold for a second. For one moment, my own sanity returned.

"Mary, this is crazy! You're very sick, do you understand me? You need help. You're starving yourself and you're not sleeping. What you're seeing isn't real. I don't know what Dr. Sparkle did to you, but I'll tell you what. Tomorrow I'm going to report him and I'm going to get you some help."

Mary, staring into the pond, oblivious, shuffling from right foot to left, scratching at her face.

"Look at the pond and think of John," she said distantly.

John? How the hell did you… No, Mary, I'm going to bed."

She didn't have to grab my wrist that time. "Think of John."

I looked into the pond again. I thought of John the way he was when we lived together. Those goddamn mints he had in glass jars all over the house. The way he could do up those striped ties of his in the most elegant Windsor knots. The splash of Glenfiddich he liked to have before bed. I thought, and then I saw. John Manson, the Cheshire cat womanizer with a pronounced window's peak and silver streaks in his hair. His face made me feel blissfully drunk. I wanted to look at him for the rest of my life.

I vaguely sensed Mary beside me, nodding and rubbing her hands together. Jesus, it was cold. It couldn't have been more than three or four degrees outside. A gust of wind sent icy ripples across that pond, and I swear that wind saved me. John's face disappeared and I left that backyard as fast as my old body could carry me.

***

Mary died a month later. I never did call a psychiatrist. How could I? How could I deny Mary what she wanted? How could I ask a psychiatrist to fix something I had seen, too? I'm glad I got the chance to understand her before she died. I understood what possessed her to rot in front of that pond. Of course, I wouldn't let it happen to me. I still woke up sometimes, hoping Mary would be at the window, inviting me to stand in front of the pond.

A few months later, some new neighbors moved in. A younger couple with a few kids. Reminded me of Mary's family a little bit. Too young and too poor to buy a proper house. I just had to go over and introduce myself. They invited me inside for a beer. We talked for a while, and somehow we got onto the topic of the pond. I'm not really sure how.

"We're going to do some landscaping here, before the winter sets in," the husband said. "I don't know what it is, but Janice and I both agree. We want that pond filled in. It just creeps us out."

I felt that old familiar ethereal pull, speaking for me. "I wouldn't do that if I were you. That pond is a good omen, though it might not feel like it. You know the old owners had a priest bless that pond?" I wasn't sure where the lie came from.

"Oh, really?" the wife said, feigning politeness. "We're not really religious folk, though."

"Don't touch that pond," I said, more firmly than I intended.

The husband nodded slowly. "Well, we'll have to discuss it, I suppose."

I smiled, trying to gloss over my desperation. "Do what you think is best. I just think you might be doing yourself a disservice, is all."

The wife asked me something about the other kids in the condo complex. She mentioned the nice green space for playing outside. I agreed, yes, it was a very nice park. I looked outside, but I wasn't looking at the park. The water felt so close. Only a few metres away.

We chatted for a while longer. They offered me another Corona, which I declined. I left shortly after.

It was funny, how the pond came up. I decided I might have to pay John one last visit before all was said and done.

The End.

Dan Thorn

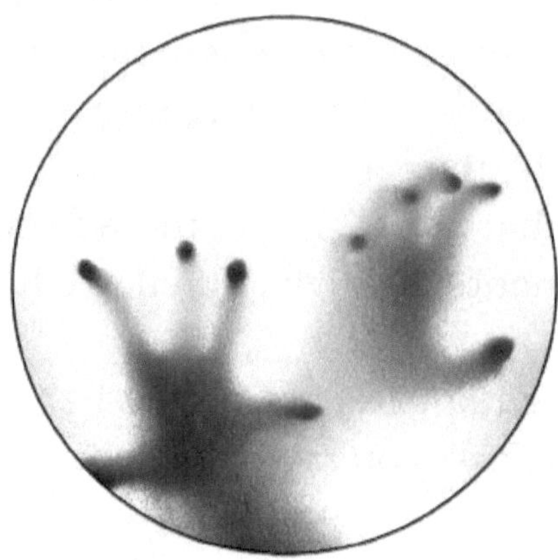

Dan Thorn lives in Calgary, Alberta. He has a B.A. in English and a J.D. in Law. He recently had another story accepted for publication in Jitter Press

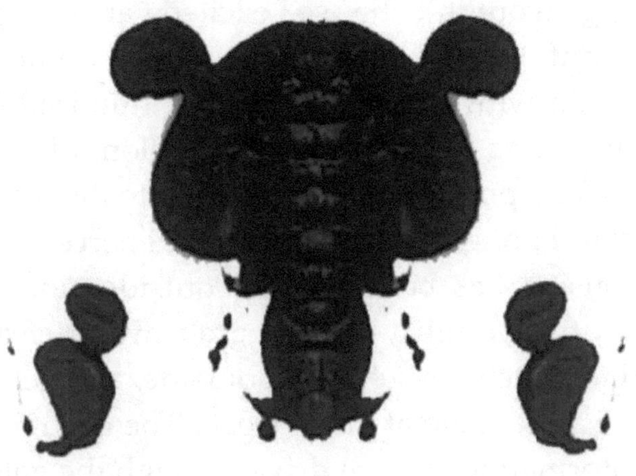

Ampu Capital by Tyler Woodsmall

Getting a client to part with something as personal as skin is a delicate conversation. I've gone over the sales pitch in my head all morning. I put on my best suit: dark black, gray-striped Oxford button-down shirt, matching tie, and a gold clip.

Usually, I wouldn't be so excited at the prospect of purchasing, but this is different. A newly-divorced Meghan Mainor has skin with a net value of four hundred million, and she has a dwindling living net of one million. I haven't felt this much elation for a purchase since I pitched to the world's leading male porn star. I bought his member for 20 percent of its value.

The limousine has been waiting outside since eleven this morning. It's twelve-thirty now. I grab my briefcase, which I handpicked to match the suit, walk outside, and get in the limo.

We arrive at her gate at one o'clock. The chauffeur gives the guard the information and we drive through the gate and down a nearly mile-long driveway.

I ring the doorbell and a woman in a maid's uniform answers. I take a deep breath and follow her into a room that sparkles with white-tiled floors, gold-rimmed mirrors, and ornate chandeliers. A perfect figure of a woman sits at a wet bar, her back to me.

"Would you like something to drink?" I've only heard her voice in films and television. It didn't sound the same.

"No." I glance at white-and-gold couches and chairs. "I'm sorry to hear about your divorce."

She turns, her drink in hand. "Is that what you're here for?"

I nod my head. Her skin is olive, with a perfect unnatural tan. Hair a thick, half-curled silvery blonde. She's nearly forty but she could pass for twenty-five.

She gestures for me to sit on one of the smaller couches. After she eases onto a chair near me, she crosses her legs. "Get on with it."

"Your stock has gone up."

She averts her eyes. "How much?"

"Triple. If you were to die tomorrow, your body would be worth over one hundred million." I grossly underestimate her net, hoping she doesn't ask for clarification.

Her blue-gray eyes grow wide. That number grabs her attention, at least enough to look at me. "That's more than my living net."

I straighten my back. "It is."

She swivels the drink in her hand ever so slightly. "I don't sell skin."

"I know. That's why I'm here." I've bought skin from hundreds of celebrities on their way down. I'm confident I can change this one's mind.

I lean back in the white silk couch. "I've heard that your divorce is becoming expensive."

"Don't believe everything you read in the tabloids."

"I don't need to read tabloids." I smile, hoping that my newly whitened teeth will give an appearance of professional poise. "If you were ever going to sell, now would be the time."

"What does that mean?"

"Your skin is worth much more without you attached to it."

Her perfectly unnatural face twists in a grimace. "You're saying that my time is up?"

"No, I'm saying that I know you need most of your skin."

One eyebrow rises into her bangs. "Most?"

I lean forward and gently take her left hand. I point to the thin, pale strip in her otherwise equal tan, imprinting where her wedding ring had been. "I know several buyers who would be interested in this. Even a couple of museums."

She stretches out her hand, examining the well-manicured finger. "How much?"

"Plenty to cover your divorce."

She takes her eyes off her hand and looks at me. "That doesn't answer my question."

"Twenty million."

"Seriously?" I can see her pupils dilate at the mention of twenty million.

"Ring fingers after a divorce have a high market value."

"Will it hurt?"

I put my briefcase on the coffee table and open it. I pull out a small, surgical, stainless-steel clipper. "Only for a moment."

Her calm sophistication turns to fidgeting in her chair and tapping her nails on the crystal glass of her drink. "The skin market is highest for a celebrity right before their career is over, isn't it?"

This is the apprehension every potential client has. "That's a rumor, a common misconception."

"Then what is the net worth of my skin based on?"

I clear my throat. "Only the fact that you are an icon." A complete lie. Desperation is key for sales. And she doesn't have the money for a lawyer.

"The skin won't be …"

She doesn't have to finish her sentence for me to know what she's asking. "I'm a licensed vendor. I can assure you consumption is off the table."

"How can you be sure?"

"It is in my best interest to make sure. I'd lose my license if your skin was ingested."

I don't mention that selling skin for consumption is a federal offense. That is a well-known fact. The argument was brought before the Supreme Court when the market became the most profitable industry of the twenty-first century.

Skin ingestion is considered prostitution by the federal government. But that isn't the real reason the law is enforced. The skin industry would've lost potential customers because skin would be deemed as a fetish market. And celebrities don't want their skin to be eaten; they want it to be admired. The law protects the industry from going down this less lucrative route.

"Are you sure it won't hurt?" Her repetition of the question tells me that pain is more of a stumbling block than the idea of losing a finger.

"I've been at this a long time. I know what I'm doing."

"I've always been against selling skin." Her voice is a whisper.

"Your ex-husband already sold his ring finger."

"He did?"

"And for a great deal less than you're being offered."

She wiggles her finger as if she wants to get more use out of it before it's gone. She takes a deep breath. "Okay."

I set the clippers down gently on the coffee table. I pull a freshly printed document from my briefcase and a sterling silver fountain pen. I present the pen to her like it was a fragile glass gift. "I'll need you to sign this bill of purchase."

She reads the paper slowly. Then signs. Her breathing comes in slow, steady inhales. "How do we do it?"

"I'll just need your hand for a moment."

From the inside pocket of my blazer, I remove a needle filled with a clear liquid. "First we numb the area."

She holds out her hand. It trembles.

"You're going to feel a slight pinch."

***

I place the finger in an airtight bag with a small amount of formaldehyde. As soon as I get home, I place the bag in a safe that doubles as a freezer.

I sit at the kitchen table and open my computer. It's been less than an hour, and the paparazzi have already taken shots of the starlet with the headline "Meghan Mainor Sells Her Ring Finger." The Financial Channel puts the skin-exchange rate at about 2 percent higher than I expected.

My phone has been ringing ever since the news broke.

For the first time in my life, I don't particularly know what I should spend the money on.

The doorbell rings. I walk through the living room and open the door.

A short, burly man with a thick beard and slicked-back hair looks up at me. "I'm here about some property you've just acquired."

I shift. "I'm sorry?"

"Meghan Mainor's finger."

My house is under a different name. Nobody is supposed to know where I live. "It will be up for sale later in the week. Get in contact with me on Friday." I begin to close the door.

The short man puts his foot between the frame and the door. "I'm afraid I'll have to insist."

I pull the door open. "Okay." Before he can get inside, I slam it on his foot and nose. With a push from the other side, the door flings me back. The air leaves my lungs in a painful exhale.

Three large men stand over me. The short one with the beard holds his face, blood covering his hand and staining his suit. "You broke my nose."

The other two men grab me and escort me to the dining room. I try to struggle, but the bald man slams me in the side of the head with his fist.

I've never been in a fight. I never realized how much a fist hurts. I'm not sure I realize it now.

Someone tapes my hands behind my back and tapes me to a chair.

My skull is empty but for the red-hot blood that leaks from my temple.

The short man pulls up a chair a few feet away from me. "I didn't get a chance to introduce myself before you so rudely slammed the door on me." He removes his right hand from his face and tastes one of his bloody fingers like he's sampling salad dressing. "I'm Walter Burrough." He points to the bald man who delivered the punch. "This here is Chris." He points to the other man, who has long black hair. "And this is … What's your name again?"

"Dom," the long-haired man says.

"That's right. As I said before, I'm here about a piece of property you've recently acquired."

I think of what I could possibly say to get myself out of this situation. "I'm sorry, gentlemen, but I can't help you."

Walter puts his finger on his nose, and with a sickening crack, he straightens it. "Are you claiming you didn't purchase Meghan Mainor's finger?"

I shake my head. "I'm saying it's not here."

Walter sniffs. "You hear that, boys? Looks like we came all this way for nothing."

The men smile.

Walter jerks out of his chair so quickly it collapses behind him. He slams both hands on the table. "I don't think you want it to go this way. Right, Alfie?"

I want to know how he knows my name. Instead of asking, I just say, "Yes."

"Well, I'm not the type to play games. So I'm just going to tell you how everything is going to go. You listening?"

I look into his cold, brown eyes.

"In case it wasn't clear from your present circumstances, you're being robbed. Now, you can accept the situation. Or you can fight back. The difference only matters to your well being."

My heart is a spasming trapeze artist and my rib cage is a tightrope. But the thought of the physical pain that I'll suffer isn't as bad as the prospect of losing a finger that's not my own. "You think I keep high-profile clients' skin here?"

Walter walks stiffly and slowly around the table and gets eye level. His nose is purple and red, and I can smell the copper in his blood. "Yes."

"Well, I don't. I put all my sales in—"

His flat hand on my cheek hurts worse than the punch.

"I'm telling the—"

Another slap. This time my face is numb enough that it doesn't sting as much.

Walter turns to his two associates. "My guess is there's a safe somewhere." He picks his chair up off the floor. "I'll just sit here with my good friend Alfie while you look."

The safe is hidden behind a panel of the wall in the upstairs office. I keep my mouth shut.

Walter puts his feet on the table and snorts. "This could've been painless, you know. But now I'm afraid it's going to be very, very painful."

I stare at his unpolished black loafers, trying not to shake. But adrenaline has set in, and fear rattles through every muscle.

"You're scared. You don't have to hide it. I've been doing this for a long time. I know what fear looks like."

I try to match his calm demeanor. "And what does it look like?"

"You."

"How did you find me?" If I'm going to die, that's the question I want answered most of all.

"People don't like you very much, Alfie. "

I scoff. "People?"

"Yeah, people, specifically some of your former clients. I hear that you once bought a cock off a porn star and sold it to a fan."

I swallow hard. "He told you?"

"Not just him. Turns out that in the skin trade, sellers remorse is prominent."

I hear loud smashing from upstairs. "They knew what they were selling."

"The way I hear it, you severely underprice the product."

I raise a shoulder. "That's just the skin business."

He laughs. "Yeah, I guess it is." Walter takes his feet off the table and crosses his arms. He sits on the edge of his chair. "At what point does buying skin become thievery?"

"I don't understand the question."

Walter holds up his hand, crusted with dried blood. "Let's say I sell you a finger, and you tell me it's worth, oh I don't know, twenty million. But it's actually worth fifty to sixty."

"I have to make a profit."

"Five million is a profit. Ten is indulgence. Thirty is theft."

A loud smash rattles the chandelier. "We found it," one of the men calls from upstairs.

Walter stands and walks to me. "Let's go look, shall we?" He cuts the tape holding me to the chair, then presses the knife against my bound hands. I feel them go free. Before I can think about fighting, he wraps an arm around my neck and puts the knife in the small of my back.

He leads me up the stairs. A voice from the safe room calls out, "In here."

Walter leads me to the room furthest down the hall on the left. My office desk lies on its side and the phone is halfway across the room, in pieces. My once well-organized paperwork is now strewn all over the floor.

Walter pushes me into the only chair in the room. The wheels project me backward, but he pulls the chair close to the safe. He touches the knife to my throat. "If you would, give us the combination."

I clench my mouth shut, wondering how far they're willing to take this.

Walter chuckles. "Know what I like about you, Alfie? You still think there's a chance you can win." He presses the knife deep enough in my skin to break it, then slides the blade up to my eye socket. The tip digs into my eye, and I choke back a sob. "You won't," he breathes into my ear.

The idea of losing the product is still more painful than the knife digging into my eye. But I can't think of any way to get out of this. "9722."

Walter nods to the long-haired man.

I hear the numbers being punched in. The safe door opens with a click. Dom hands Walter the airtight bag.

"Meghan Mainor's finger. How much do you reckon it's worth?"

"Retail, you could get about sixty-two million."

He holds up the bag. "And how much did you buy it for?"

Remembering what he said about profit, I don't speak.

He lowers the bag and glares at me. "Choose your answer wisely, Alfie. I already know what you paid for it. But I want to hear you say it."

"Twenty million," I choke out.

He laughs. "That's a bit of an under-sale."

He slides the knife to my crotch. I can feel the sharp sting through my trousers. I suck in air as if that will stop the pain.

"You know why a washed-up celebrity is worth more dead than alive?"

I look at the finger. "Skin net is based—"

He puts up his hand. "It was a rhetorical question. What good is currency if it is never exchanged?"

I don't answer.

"That question wasn't rhetorical."

"Nothing."

He jumps forward but not menacingly. His grin is manic but genuine. "Right! That's absolutely correct. If currency isn't up for exchange, it's worthless. That's why celebrities who have lost their earning power are worth more in the skin market."

"What's your point?"

"How many celebrities have you bought from?"

My skin is crawling. "I couldn't put a number on it."

He cuts open the bag with the finger inside. He walks toward me with it. "You know, Alfie, I'd hoped you would have recognized me by now."

I study his face, his body. For a moment, a sickening twist of familiarity creeps into my stomach, but it's gone in a flash.

"Maybe this will help jog your memory." He drops the knife to the ground and unzips his pants with his free hand. With his trousers around his ankles, I can make out a lump of conjoined flesh. The space between his legs is empty except for the mangled scar.

He points to Dom, who pulls back his long hair, revealing the place where his left ear would be, now a scar.

I barely remember that job.

I try to dart out of the room, but the bald man grabs me and throws me back into the rolling chair. He stands over me and opens his mouth. He pulls back his cheeks, revealing he has no tongue.

Walter takes the bald man's place. "You remember now?"

The nervous tension dissipates into sepulchral certainty. "I remember the incisions and the products. But I don't remember you."

Walter grimaces. "I guess you wouldn't. Celebrities come and go."

He wraps his free hand around my face and pushes my head back, squeezing my cheeks. "Open your mouth."

I clench my teeth.

He forces my mouth open, then shoves Meghan Mainor's cold, damp finger into it.

He clamps my jaw shut. "How much will it be worth if you chew it up and swallow it?"

My eyes water as the taste makes me gag.

He loosens his grip. "That wasn't rhetorical either."

The finger bobs like a loose piece of gristle at the back of my throat. Sixty million dollars taste like salt and chemical preservative, for some reason I imagined it would taste different.

I try to think of an answer to his question that can somehow save me, but there isn't one. "Nothing."

His broken nose is inches from my face. He's breathing heavy. I can feel his heartbeat through his hand on my cheeks.

"Start chewing."

The End.

Tyler Woodsmall

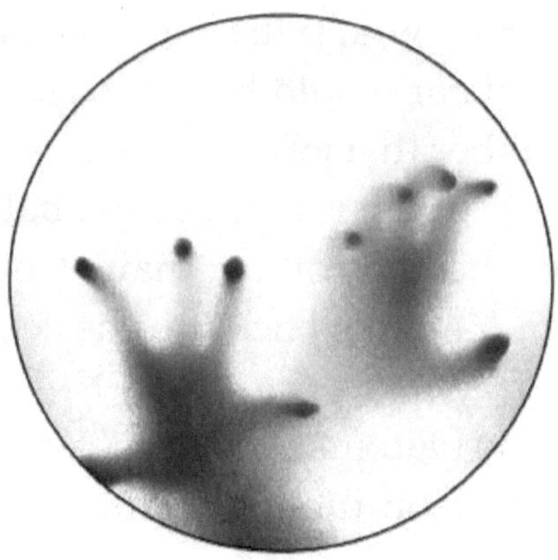

Tyler Woodsmall attends Goddard College, where he is the current managing editor for the undergraduate BFA literary journal Duende. He lives above an Indian restaurant in a room with no windows in Brooklyn.

Review by Heaven of Horror of The Caretaker

The Caretaker is a creepy tale with some nice plot developments and a crazy old lady at the center of it all.

Watching the trailer is always a good indication for most movies, but The Caretakerdelivers so much more than you would expect. Of course, the one thing from the trailer that you will get to enjoy is Sondra Blake playing her heart out as the older lady with shady intentions.

To be fair, I have to admit that I first thought the supporting character of August was annoying and preppy in the worst way. He plays the boyfriend of the old lady's granddaughter, so he's a pretty big part of the story. As it turns out, he is actually a very interesting character and Sean Martini portrays him perfectly. So much so, that I almost felt bad for disliking him at first.

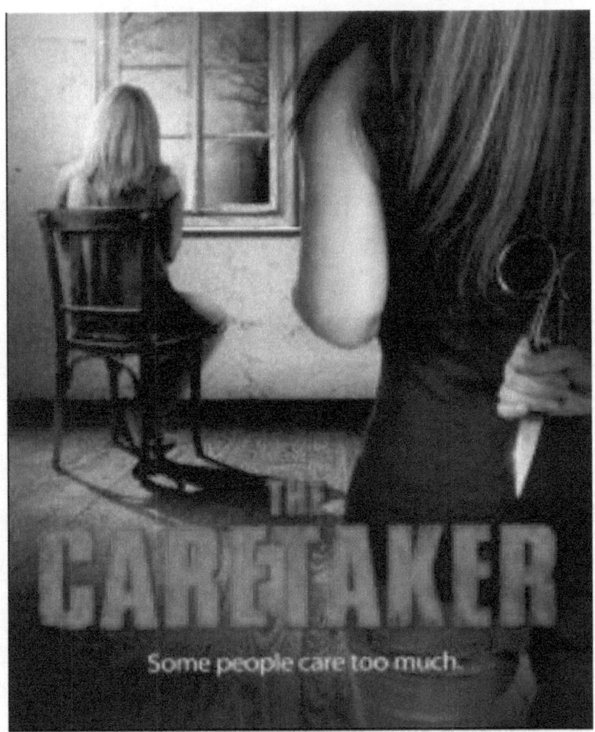

What I really took away from watching The Caretaker is the fact that a great story or great characters can carry a movie, but when you have both, the magic begins to happen. There's no huge budget behind this movie, but you won't think about that while watching it. Both sound and images are crisp, so your focus will remain on the story.

Also, they manage to give you some real insight into several of the characters, which is no small feat for a movie with a runtime of just 80 minutes. Then again, this is exactly what's possible, when you take away all the stereotypical scenes. Even the obligatory horror movie sex scene won't play out as you expect!

I'll gladly rave about the good story, interesting characters and perfect pace of The Caretaker, but really, you should watch this movie for Sondra Blake. There's a scene where she's just dancing around in some sort of trance, and I could've watched that for the longest time. She is so damn intense and honest, which will freak you out! She's the biggest sweetheart towards her granddaughter, Mallorie, while almost hissing at the boyfriend. And she's not some creeper pretending to like him when Mallorie is there. Oh no, she's pretty brutal and direct all the time.

In case the name Sondra Blake sounds familiar, but you can't quite place it, I can tell you she was in the 1976 movie Helter Skelter (about Charles Manson). She's also guest-starred in lots of TV shows, and yes, she was previously married to Robert Blake.

Even though Sondra Blake is very memorable, the rest of the cast is amazing as well. From Meegan Warner, who is the actual star of the movie, to Barry Jenner (Star Trek: Deep Space Nine) and Chanel Celaya. Both have small but important roles. You might recognize Chanel Celaya from a small role in the 21 Jump Street movie or the "Gravel to Tempo" music video from Hayley Kioko. Celaya became Tumblr famous almost immediately as "headphones girl". In fact, someone made a blog just for that small music video character! And of course, Sean Martini is excellent as the boyfriend, August.
A new horror duo?

Jeff Prugh directed the movie, which is his debut directing a feature film alone. He co-directed Leave of Absence back in 2013 and did four short films prior to that one. Based on The Caretaker, I certainly hope he'll do more in this genre, cause it really works very well with him at the helm. The script was by Jeremy Robinson, who also wrote one of the short films Jeff Prugh has done. In fact, those are the two scripts Jeremy Robinson has enjoyed seeing produced. Maybe this is a new horror duo to follow? I'll definitely be ready to watch whatever either of them come out with next... and yes, my expectations are set accordingly.

The Caretaker is out in US theaters on September 30.

-*-*-

ScreamQueen:

Sometimes a chosen name seems to stick, but it's no secret that my real name is Karina Adelgaard. I write reviews and recaps on HeavenofHorror.com and yes, it does happen that I find myself screaming, when watching a good horror movie. I love psychological horror, survival horror, and kick-ass women. Also, I have a huge soft spot for a good horror-comedy. Oh yeah, and I absolutely HATE when animals are harmed in movies, so I will immediately think less of any movie, where animals are harmed for entertainment (even if the animals are just really good actors). Fortunately, horror doesn't use this nearly as much as comedy. And people assume horror lovers are the messed-up ones. Go figure!

HorrorDiva:

My real name is Nadja Houmøller, but the name HorrorDiva just seems to work for me. I usually keep up-to-date with all the horror news, and make sure Heaven of Horror share the best and latest trailers for upcoming horror movies. I love all kinds of horror. My love affair started when I watched 'Poltergeist' alone around the age

81

of 10. I slept like a baby that night and I haven't stopped watching horror movies since. The crazy slasher stuff isn't really for me, but hey, to each their own. I guess I just like to be scared and get jump scares, more than being disgusted and laughing at the grotesque. Also, Korean and Spanish horror movies made within the past 10-15 years are among my absolute favorites.

Does It Make a Sound? by Kevin Buchholz

Nancy and Victor Galloway trudged along Hallman's Pass, the air dense with the scent of rain. Grey light filtered in through the tree canopy above, casting an ethereal glow on the underbrush and moss nearby. They'd set out from their campsite earlier that morning in hopes of reaching The Falls by mid-afternoon, but Hallman's Pass quickly proved more difficult to traverse than Victor's guidebook suggested. What had been described as "a quick shortcut to The Falls from Green Valley campgrounds" was more of a thin dirt strip winding through the backwoods and mountainous terrain of the nearby Adirondacks.

"Vic," Nancy panted as they stepped over a hollowed-out and rotting log in their path, "Let's just go back. We should have seen something by now. It's almost three-thirty." Victor turned and eyed his wife briefly. Sweat clung to her face and held her bangs down across her forehead.

"Just thirty minutes, ok? Just a half-hour. If we don't hear running water by then, we can turn back." He replied. He didn't want to turn back at all and was sure that they'd come across The Falls or the main hiking paths they'd forsaken earlier. His guide book warned that those paths clogged-up with tourists and weekend warriors throughout the summer months, and Victor hated crowds.

"Come on, Vic! We're not getting anywhere!" Nancy snapped. Victor read her tone and deciphered that she'd been masking impatience and frustration for at least an hour or two now. If they didn't come across something soon she'd mentally lock down and they wouldn't speak until they got back in the car on Tuesday; he could kiss his dreams of anniversary sex in a tent goodbye.

"Nancy..."

"No!" She stopped in her tracks. "We should have seen something by now! The book said there were overlook spots, right? Looking down on the river?"

"Yeah, but-"

"I haven't even heard the river, Vic. Have you? We've been hiking since eight and I haven't heard running water once!"

Victor felt anger rise in his voice. He recognized the underlying accusatory message building in Nancy's words. Somehow this was his fault, and if it wasn't yet it would be soon. He had to calm her nerves or he risked a Nancy meltdown…or worse, a Victor meltdown.

"What do you want me to do, Nance? What? We haven't seen anything. You're right. I don't know what the deal is."

"I want us to turn around. If we start now we can make it back to the valley by sunset." She offered, her words holding an air of compromise.

"Nancy, I just have a feeling that it can't be much further. We've been walking too long to not find anything, so it can't be much further."

"But the guidebook said –"

"The guidebook is thirty fucking years old, Nancy!" Victor spurted, his eyes open wide. He immediately rued the outburst and his words came louder than he'd meant them to. Nancy frowned slightly and opened her mouth to let out a silent *tsk*.

"Take me back. Now." She ordered.

Victor wiped sweat from his brow and glanced down at the dirt trail.

"Look…look, I'm sorry. I didn't mean to snap at you –"

"Victor, I don't care. I don't care about The Falls; I don't care about this trip. I just want to go back to the campground and then I want to go home in the morning."

She's locking up. Fucking great. Victor thought. A surge of red-fury washed over him and he curled his right hand into a fist, but the anger wiped away in another instant. He approached Nancy and opened his arms, placing his hands on her bare shoulders. She looked away and shrugged one hand off.

"I'm sorry. We'll go back now." Nancy turned and looked into his eyes. Her expression indicated surprise and hinted at disbelief; Victor usually put up more of a fight than this. For a brief instant, she suspected that he held an ulterior motive, but Victor's face revealed mental exhaustion.

"Are you all right, Vic?"

"Let's just go. I don't want to fight with you – I just wanted a good anniversary."

Nancy sighed inwardly and took his hands in hers.

"This is a good anniversary." She stood on her toes and kissed him softly. "Now come on. If the spot we camped in last night is still open, we can make it a *really* good anniversary."

***

They marched back along Hallman's Pass, the slate-grey light falling slightly darker as the afternoon dragged on. A light breeze ruffled the leaves overhead, the only sound they could hear aside from the chirping of a few birds out of sight.

"When was it your dad came here, again?" Nancy asked. She now led the two of them down the thin dirt trail.

"Jeez, I don't know…" Victor responded, "Had to have been in the 80s. It was right after he and my mom got divorced – one of his "finding himself" trips. His pictures of The Falls were from that trip, I think. Or the next one. I'm not sure."

They trudged on for another hour, the light fading much faster than considered normal for July in upstate New York. Nancy picked up her pace without realizing it. Victor gazed into the tree canopy, searching for the birds singing in the distance, but found none.

"I didn't really notice on the way in, but there's really nothing to see on this path at all."

"How could you not notice?" Nancy replied, a faint signature of disgust peppering her words.

"I mean, I noticed, but I didn't pay attention to it I guess. I honestly don't think many people use this path much at all. You'd expect to see some garbage bins or something. This is a state park."

"Well, maybe it was too expensive to keep up," Nancy suggested. Her tone grew weary again. Victor chose his words carefully.

"It's possible," he agreed, "But if they closed it down there would have been a sign blocking it in the first place. I mean, it did say "Hallman's Pass" when we came in, right?"

"Yes, dear, but maybe the "closed" sign fell down or something. I don't know. It doesn't matter now."

"Oh well," Victor offered. He didn't want her to turn on him now. His shirt collar, underarms, and lower back showed expanding circles of sweat and he could see the same on Nancy. Victor estimated another two hours of hiking, three tops, and he was almost certain they were going downhill.

Nancy suddenly looked up, a pang of alarm slicing through her body.

"I don't remember a fork in the road."

***

Hallman's Pass split off to the left and right, an acute angle of about thirty degrees separating the paths at the crux. Both appeared to lead West and cut through equal amounts of thick forest. The birds above had slowed their incessant chorus, the only performers left seeming to be some ways off.

"Maybe we just didn't see it. I was looking ahead the entire time." Victor said, face fixed in a confused frown.

"There was no fork, Vic. The path was straight the entire way!" Nancy replied, raising her voice slightly.

"Ok, just calm down."

"Don't tell me to calm down! I don't want to get lost out here! This isn't my idea of a good time!" She retorted.

"We're not going to get lost, Jesus. It's 2016." Victor muttered. A small levy in his brain cracked.

"Yeah, and our phones don't work out here, genius!"

"Nancy," Victor gritted his teeth, "We have the guidebook, and – "

"Oh, we're ok! We have a guidebook! A thirty-year-old guidebook! What does it say about the fork in the road, Victor?" Her voice bordered on full-blown shouts.

"We're in a fucking state park, Nancy! It's real hard to get lost in a state park!"

"Well, somehow you managed to do that! Christ!"

The flares of anger surged back, crashing in small waves on the shore of Victor's musculature. He forced himself to take deep breaths and remember his therapy. Nancy continued.

"I don't know why the hell I agreed to this trip, in the first place. I wanted to go to the beach, but no! No, we can't go to the beach in the summer! It'll be too crowded and too hot! Isn't that what you said?"

"Nancy, you're really starting to piss me off. I'm asking you nicely – "

"You're asking me nicely?" Nancy frowned in disbelief. "Or what? Or what, Vic?! Are you threatening me?"

"No, I'm just telling you that I'm really struggling right now and I'd appreciate it if you'd stop."

"Five grand on therapy sessions and you're telling me *now* that you're struggling? Are you *fucking* joking!?" She yelled, and when she did, his fist clenched in an almost auto-response.

"Nancy," Victor growled, "Please."

"Please!? You promised me, Victor! You promised me! Were you lying?!"

"I didn't lie to you!" Victor countered, his anger simmering inside the clenched fist.

"You did! You lied to me!"

"I didn't lie, you bitch!" Victor exploded, his lips pulled back in a snarl. He swung his fist outwards, pulling it away from Nancy with all his willpower and striking a nearby tree. Bark splintered upon its impact and scattered in small chunks on the forest floor. Thin trickles of blood ran from Victor's fingers, though he felt nothing. He stood and stared into Nancy's terrified eyes, shaking and breathing heavily.

Nancy stared back, stunned. She seemed to shrink into the foliage around her, eyes shocked and mouth frozen in silence. Victor crouched and cradled his head in his hands. With glazed-over vision, he focused on the dirt path below. Guilt overwhelmed him and anchored his gaze to the forest floor. He'd made it eighteen months with no outbursts until now.

"I'm…I'm sorry." He muttered. A full three minutes of silence greeted the apology. "Nance…Nance? I'm really sorry." He glanced up. Nancy stood in the same position, her sight locked in the distance. Victor stood up, slowly reaching out to her shoulder. He lowered his hand for a moment, the thin trickles of blood drying in reddish-brown hues on his skin, then lifted it again and tapped Nancy's shoulder.

"Hnng!" Nancy gasped, jerking her head and pulling instinctively away from Victor in the process. She trembled and pulled her arms inward, hugging herself. Victor silently sighed and dropped to a knee in front of her.

"Listen…I'm…we're both stressed and tired and I let it get the best of me. You know I don't want…I would never hurt…I'm sorry, Nancy. I don't know what else I can say."

Nancy's paralysis dissolved from her face, replaced by fault-lines of deep, underlying resentment. The look terrified Victor, placing him in a mental-defensive stance. He awaited an onslaught of ultimatums, threats, and insults – all of which he'd become familiar with prior to therapy – but Nancy responded quietly with a few short words instead.

"Get me out of here."

Not a request. A command.

***

The Galloways shuffled down the left-hand path, Victor rationalizing that the right path must diverge Northwest at some point and thus would never have started in the Green Valley campgrounds to begin with.

Nancy moved in silence behind Victor, speaking solely in positive and negative affirmation grunts when addressed by her husband. They crossed fallen logs, over mossy rocks, and under an ever-darkening canopy of trees above. The birds fell still, the only noises now coming from an occasional soft breeze and the crunch of their boots on twigs.

After two hours of further trudging, the threat of oncoming night and the slow-panic tailing behind it encapsulated their surroundings. Victor thought he recognized the path's various landmarks (tree clusters and rocks) in the first thirty minutes of walking it, but this fled with the light. Their pace quickened, an invisible side-effect of their mutual desire to leave the forest and return to their creature comforts. The physical distance between him and Nancy melted in small increments with each step until she finally took his hand and they marched on in silence, two anxious lovers lost in the woods.

"We have to stop." He reluctantly said.

"I know." She replied. It was an answer he hadn't expected, but was welcomed.

"We won't be able to see in another fifteen or twenty minutes and I don't think either of us wants to sprain a leg out here."

"No." She answered. "How about we set the tent up right over there?" Nancy pointed to a small patch of relatively clear ground amongst the trees to their left.

"Yeah. Yeah that's fine. Help me unpack it?"

With that, they constructed their small abode for the evening. Victor had recently purchased it from Wal-Mart on sale for this very trip, choosing this model based on online user reviews for its excellent water-proof lining. The original plan to set up shop by The Falls would have made this feature handy, though now he was just pleased to have shelter from the oncoming night. It bothered him more than he would ever admit that they had somehow managed to lose themselves on an old dirt path. Nancy addressed the issue herself shortly after the two of them climbed inside, zipping both the mesh-screen and outer doors to the tent and sealing themselves off from the forest.

"Are we going to be ok?" She asked with childlike apprehension and innocence. Victor unfurled his sleeping bag next to hers and glanced her way, her face beautiful in the light of the large flashlight hanging from the roof of the tent on a lone hook.

"Of course." He responded. "We're just a little lost. I think we got too hot and too tired and we bit off more than we could chew." He pulled his shirt off, tossing its sweat-soaked glory to the corner of the tent near their backpacks. "Are you ok?"

"Yeah." Nancy answered, and for the first time that day, he believed her. She lifted her shirt off and tossed it to the corner as well. Victor rolled over to her side of the tent and the two embraced, comforted in their makeshift shelter. Nancy leaned up and kissed her husband lightly on the forehead, then leaned back and removed her sports-bra. Her breasts fell out invitingly and she guided his hands to them.

***

They made love for an hour. Both internally agreed that it was the best they'd had in some time as they lay spooning in the tent, the flashlight above now turned off. They spoke softly to one another in the darkness, conversation light and meaningless, each in a world of complete relaxation. Nancy sighed.

"How far do you think we have left tomorrow?" she asked. Victor kissed her neck and cradled his chin in the nook between it and her shoulder.

"An hour or two tops. It took us five or six on the way out and we've nearly hit that already. But who knows," he said in a melodramatic, Vincent Price-esque attempt to be spooky, "Maybe we'll be walking all daaaaay!" Nancy smacked him on the thigh and smiled in the dark. The two lay still for a moment.

"Listen," Nancy began, "About…about earlier –"

"You can leave me if it happens again. You didn't deserve that." Nancy turned and faced her husband.

"It's not that, Vic. I mean, you scared me, but it goes further. I think you need –"

Snap.

Nancy breathed in sharply and sat up.

"What the fuck was that?" She whispered in the dark tent. Her heartbeat accelerated tenfold.

"Something outside," Victor whispered back, "Probably a squirrel. Chill out." Victor put an arm around her and chuckled, his shoulders heaving with each laugh. She eased into his chest.

"I'm sorry, I just…I'm on edge today. I can't wait to get –"

Snap snap SNAP.

The sounds of twigs and underbrush cracking on the forest floor flooded into the tent, muffled slightly from the water-proof barrier between the interior and the outside. Soft thuds approached the zip-up door. Nancy's grip on her husband held strong.

"That's not a fucking squirrel, Victor!" She whispered, her voice shrill and nervous.

"Shhhh!" He hissed back. They lied in total silence, each with ears perked to the music of the night. Victor leaned to his wife's ear and murmured, almost noiselessly, "It might be a bear. Stay quiet. We'll be fine." He reached up and unhooked their flashlight from its spot as a makeshift chandelier and held it by their side.

"What do we do if it gets in?" Nancy asked, now trembling.

"Nancy, you have to be quiet," he whispered, "we don't have open food with us so it should just go –"

"Victor?" A voice sliced through the night outside. Nancy froze in place and Victor's chest seized up. "Victor, is that you? Are you in there?"

The electric anxiety coursing between them dissipated into confusion and Victor switched the flashlight on. He and Nancy exchanged perplexed glances.

Victor Galloway recognized the voice outside.

***

"Victor, it's Mike, Mike Hunter." the voice kept on. Victor frowned and Nancy mouthed Mike Hunter's name to him, punctuating it with a question mark.

"Mike?" He stated, looking for an answer in his words though finding none that made sense.

"Yeah, it's me." The voice responded, the sounds of exhaustion and chattering teeth filtering through as well.

"What, uh…what are you doing out here, Mike?" Victor asked, reaching for the zipper to the tent's main door.

"I'm camping with my wife and the kids, remember? I told you last week." Victor's thumb and index finger gripped the zipper tightly as his brain worked to recall this. He vaguely remembered the conversation. "Vic? Are you there?"

"Yeah, Mike, I'm here, I just don't…is something wrong?" Nancy frowned towards her husband. Victor dropped his hand from the zipper.

"Yeah…well, I don't know. It's my wife, I…I can't find her…I can't find the kids. I don't know where they are, they aren't in the tent!" Mike's voice wavered, riddled with panic. Victor turned and exchanged confused glances with Nancy. "I went out to take a piss and I came back and the tent was open and everything was gone! Just gone! I'm really scared Vic, I don't even know –"

"Ok, Mike, ok, just hold on." Victor reached back for the zipper.

A sudden lurching force shook the sleeping bag behind Victor and in an instant, he felt Nancy's arm shoving him away from the zipper. Victor's grip slipped away and he glanced down at his wife, her eyes stern with apprehension and swimming in fear.

93

"Vic? Is Nancy with you? Is that Nancy?" Mike asked, his voice shaking. Nancy shook her head silently, mouthing "No" to her husband.

"Uh...uh, yeah, Mike, yeah she's here. Mike, listen –"

"Nancy, please, I need your help! I need both your help, I can't find them!" Mike pleaded.

"How did you find us out here, Mike?" Nancy asked, suspicion clear in her tone. Victor looked between her and the tent door. A moment of silence lingered all around them.

"I recognized the tent. Vic was talking about it at work, said he'd just bought it. He said the waterproof lining would be good for The Falls – how is that important?! My family is missing! Please, I need your help! My daughter is asthmatic and her inhaler was on the tent floor!" Panic rose in Mike's voice again and simultaneously burned across Vic's face. He scrambled towards his backpack and began rooting inside it.

"Mike, you didn't answer my question," Nancy responded, "How did you know we were here specifically? We haven't seen anyone all day. I'm sure a lot of people have this tent."

"I, eh, what?! Nancy, are you joking right now?" cried Mike, his voice growing indignant. "I saw your tent and I thought it might be you and Victor! Why are you acting like I'm crazy?! Why are we wasting all this time!? My family is gone! I need your help and you're acting like I'm crazy!" Victor drew a small notepad and a pen from his backpack and began scribbling furiously.

"We're not, Mike, I promise," Nancy replied, "It's just a little strange that...well..."

"Well, what?!" Mike asked, subtle drops of anger tinting his words. Goosebumps raised across Nancy's arms and shoulders. "Hello? Hello!?" Suddenly, Victor shoved the notepad into Nancy's hands. She glanced down at it and felt her calves fill with lead.

It read, "Mike Hunter has twin sons – he doesn't have a daughter!"

"Victor? Nancy? Hello!?" Mike called. "Talk to me, what's wrong? We're wasting time, please!" The panic in his voice transformed with each word, growing increasingly hollow and almost melodramatic.

"Uh…Mike, listen, it's late. Why don't you find a park ranger and tell them what you told us?" Victor offered. Nancy withdrew to the center of the tent, her eyes confused and afraid. Victor took her hand, his heartbeat increasing.

"Don't you think I already tried that? They don't believe me!"

"Well, Mike, that doesn't make sense. That's their job. Why wouldn't they —-"

"I don't fucking know, Vic! How the fuck should I know! Ugh! We're not getting anywhere!" Mike yelled at the tent door. Nancy's chest seized from within, her ears detecting a split in the sound of Mike's voice for a fraction of a second. It was as if two tones erupted from Mike's throat: one normal, one empty and deep. The same momentary paralysis struck Victor's throat, his vocal cords struggling to voice a reply.

"Mike, I'm sorry, it's just you're not making a lot of sense, and —"

"My family could be hurt, Vic! What don't you fucking understand about that?!"

"Calm down, Mike! It's not going to do anything for us to walk around the forest in the dark, we'll get lost!"

"Pft! Some fucking friend you are! You fucking asshole! Both of you!"

Victor hesitantly reached for the zipper on the tent door once more. A hard squeeze on his left hand from Nancy stopped him. An almost infinite moment of silence grasped the air around them, and was broken as suddenly as it had arrived. Shrugs and grumbles of anger and dissatisfaction carried from outside into the tent, twigs snapping in conjunction with them. Nancy silently sighed as Mike's footsteps led away into the forest. Victor turned to her, hugging her around the shoulder.

"He's gone."

"That was really fucking weird, Vic." She whispered. "How do you know that guy? I don't think I've even met him."

"I'm sure you have, he was at the Christmas party last year. He's the head IT guy for the whole office. It's just…I don't know, something –"

A sudden and rapid series of thudding footsteps exploded outward from the forest, culminating in a rage-filled roar and the shaking of the tent all around Victor and Nancy. The flashlight hanging from the tent ceiling dropped to the floor, casting a yellow-white circle on the nylon tent door.

"You fucken assholes! They're gonna die out there and it's all your fault! It's all your fucking fault!" Mike screamed. Nancy joined suit, kicking herself backwards to the rear wall. Victor reflexively dropped back with her, then lunged forward to pick up the flashlight. Foot-sized impressions dented the nylon door as Mike kicked it, returning the door to its normal shape each time his heel retreated. Deep-red splotches of anger began dotting Victor's vision, another episode imminent as adrenaline now found its way into his system. He lurched forward and gripped the zipper on the door again, Nancy grabbing his arm once more and pleading with him, her voice in hysterics.

"No! Vic don't! Please don't!"

"I'm gonna break his fucking nose!" He yelled, shrugging Nancy off. His muscles applied downward force to the zipper as Mike continued his tantrum outside.

"Get out here, you piss-ant!"

The deep, black, pungent odor of rot cut through the air inside the tent like a guillotine and stopped Victor's door opening-motion dead in its tracks. He gagged and immediately covered his nose, Nancy doing the same. Mike spoke again.

"What the fuck are you waiting for!? Huh!?" The rage inhabiting Mike's voice had inexplicably disappeared and was now overflowing with a dark cynicism. The dual-pitch Nancy identified for a fleeting moment earlier now inhabited each word. A subtle din of dark, agonizing voices crept into and enveloped the air surrounding the tent in a language neither Victor nor Nancy had heard before, sapping all confidence from them both. Nancy whimpered.

"Where are you, big man?! Huh?" Mike taunted, a sadistic beckoning in his tone. Victor opened his mouth to speak but found that no words would escape his throat. Nancy's grip on his arm grew so tight that it felt prickly, the blood circulating inside coming to a halt.

"M...Mike...you don't have a daughter." Victor croaked, his mouth throat dry and gravely. The voices growing in a black, malevolent fervor around the tent came to an immediate halt. Victor's voice dropped to a barely audible whisper. "Who are you?"

Silence.

***

Hysterical laughter suddenly erupted from the outside of the tent, Mike's words struggling in between chuckles.

"I had you going there, didn't I?" He asked. "Oh man, I can only imagine what your face looks like right now, hahahaha!" Nancy and Victor exchanged glances, Victor frowning and shaking his head, Nancy still frightened but now more confused. "Hahaha, oh man, that was too good. Anyway, my family's fine – we're set up over in Green Valley. I came out here for some firewood and saw the tent — figured I'd see if it was you, maybe give you a scare! I think I did pretty well!"

Nancy exchanged confused glances with her husband, mouthing "what" to him in silence?

"You sure fucking did, Mike...Jesus," Victor responded. Adrenaline still ran wild in his veins but his heartbeat slowed from a gallop to a brisk walk.

"Mike?" Nancy asked, trembling slightly though breathing more easily.

"Yeah, Nancy?"

"How far are we from the campgrounds? We couldn't see them from the path."

"Eh, I'd say about five minutes away, not far at all. If you two stuck to the trail a little further you'd be there right now." Victor glanced at Nancy with an "I told you so" look plastered on his face. Nancy sighed deeply, lowering herself back down on the sleeping bag and covering her eyes. "Why don't you two come to our site for a bit? We're going to make s'mores and tell ghost stories to the kids!" Victor lay down next to his wife.

"I think we've had enough scares for one night, Mike, thanks. Maybe we'll stop by in the morning on our way out." Victor said, slipping his left hand into the grip of his wife's right.

"Aw come on, was I really that spooky?" Mike asked.

"Goodnight, Mike." Victor replied, his voice marked with finality.

"Haha, all right, goodnight guys." Mike chuckled, his footsteps moving further and further away until they couldn't be heard anymore.

Nancy turned to Victor and the two embraced tightly, their breathing relaxing again.

"Who does that? Really?" Nancy whispered.

"I don't know. Let's just try to get some rest and get out of here in the morning." Victor replied, his eyes closed.

"But his voice, Vic. How the hell did he do that?"

"Nancy, please, can we just sleep now? Please?"

Nancy dropped her gaze and eased out of the embrace. She sighed and turned away from her husband, simultaneously reaching for her cell phone. She tapped its screen and it lit up dimly, showing 10:30 PM on its timestamp, but there was still no semblance of a signal to be found. She lowered the phone and closed her eyes tightly.

Sleep did not come to Nancy Galloway. The physical stress of the day echoed in all of her muscles, small brushfires of aches burning lightly, but not small enough to die on their own. Victor's breathing had slowed and now came deeply and gently, always on the verge of snoring but never crossing over the barrier. Nancy's mind raced, focusing mostly on Mike. She couldn't figure out why he'd target them like that or how he pulled off the sounds he made.

And that smell. What the hell was that smell? It was almost like something –

Died.

That was it.

She knew she had smelled it before. It was during the fall of 1987, Nancy then just the young daughter of Phil and Lily Hartman, a blue-collar couple living in Madison, Wisconsin. Phil enjoyed many of life's simple pleasures, mostly Wisconsin Badger football, Green Bay Packer football, and beer, but deer hunting was his all-around favorite pastime. He'd always hoped to share this with a son, but after Nancy's birth that was impossible – Lily was unable to bear any more. It disappointed him slightly, but Phil loved his daughter unconditionally and tried to make her interested in everything he liked. His efforts showed mixed results, but deer hunting was the only one-hundred percent failure of them all.

They set out on a cold, infinitely grey November morning, the roads still covered in slush from a week of light and entirely too-early snow. Donning their camouflage jackets and bright orange safety vests, Nancy and her father set out into the woods to track their kill, purposefully moving against the wind.

The wind itself brought the stench, a horrible aroma that glued itself into Nancy's nasal cavities for weeks after. The two marched twenty or so yards Northeast to the source of the rot, the carcasses of two fawns, one seemingly ripped in half with its rib cage broken and exposed, the other missing a large chunk of flesh from its neck. Dried blood matted what remained of their fur, clinging tightly to their bone structure. The stench of decay pervaded the kill site.

The sight of animal corpses had never bothered Nancy before – her father brought home his prey all the time during hunting season and the family would make as much use of the meat as possible – but this was different. The vulgarity of what was on display shattered what remained of her childhood innocence, and she didn't need her father's words to let her know that the wounds on these fawns were not the result of a human being. Nancy saw the unbridled wrath of nature in those carcasses and smelled death itself –horrible, rancid death.

***

The memory of the dead fawns flashed through her mind once again when she heard the first thud. Nancy's eyes shot open and she reached for her phone once more, now reading 12:07 AM. Another thud came, sounding roughly fifty feet away in the direction of the tent door. It was a heavy noise, resonating on a deep, sub-level one could feel within the body.

Footsteps? Nancy thought, her heartbeat now coming fast again. *They have to be.* She turned and shook Victor's shoulders. His breathing abruptly left its comfort zone and he blinked his eyes open, confused as to his location.

"Vic! Wake up, wake up! Listen! Listen! Do you hear it?"

Victor continued blinking.

"Nancy, what are –" he began, then stopped. The thuds moved closer and closer, now only twenty or so feet from the tent door. Victor frowned angrily, everything clicking in his mind.

"Oh, that's it," Victor growled, "That fucker's dead. I'm sick of this bullshit."

"Victor, don't you dare open that door!" Nancy said, voice rising in the dark of the tent. Vic was already sitting up and switching the flashlight on. He reached for his hiking boots as the thuds drew nearer.

"I'm done, Nancy! I'm done!" He responded impatiently, tying the first boot.

"You're done?" Mike's voice asked from behind them. Nancy and Victor both jumped backwards towards the tent door, Nancy screaming in surprise. Mike had to be standing directly on the other side of the rear tent wall in both of their minds, but the thuds drew closer to the door.

"Mike, this isn't fucking funny! This isn't cute!" Victor yelled. Laughter greeted them from the rear of the tent.

"I agree with you, Victor. It's not." Mike replied, now at the tent door. Victor and Nancy jerked their heads in its direction, unknowingly inching closer to one another. "I wish you would have come out with me before. We could have had so much fun. I don't get to have much fun nowadays." Footsteps thudded around the tent in circles from rear to front, branches and underbrush crunching beneath them. Each thud reverberated in Nancy and Victor's chest, heavy and dreadful. "You can still come out here on your own, you know. It would save us both a lot of trouble."

"Who the fuck are you?" Victor growled, attempting to bring out the rage-filled alpha male within but finding no confidence. His words arrived empty. Nancy's eyes followed the sounds of the footsteps, her legs filling with lead once more.

"Who am I?" The voice outside answered. "I'm Mike, of course."

"You aren't Mike! Who the fuck are you!?" Nancy yelled.

A chorus of low, mournful cries raised again in the distance.

"No? No, I suppose I'm not Mike. But what difference does it make? Why not just come see for yourself who I am?"

"We're not coming out there! No way!" Victor called out as he shined the flashlight at all the tent walls chaotically.

Suddenly, a loud and heavy intake of air whooshed above the tent, as if wind was breathed into a large set of cancerous lungs.

"I like your smell." The voice spoke above them, its twin-toned natured returned. "That's how I found you in the first place. It's how I always find your kind. Your blood stinks...but it's so nice."

"What do you want from us!?" Nancy yelled, her lungs straining as tears fell down her face. Victor shivered, the tent interior now extremely cold.

"I just want to talk to you...talk to you out here." The voice replied, the scent of putrefaction and feces accompanying it, slicing the frigid air inside. Nancy gagged twice, the taste of bile rising through her throat before abruptly lowering. Not as lucky, Victor vomited a mixture of water and half-digested power bars onto the tent floor.

"Victor!" Nancy cried, pulling her husband towards her and wiping chunks of spit and granola from his lower-lip. "Oh, God!"

"That is a name with no power here," the voice spoke, the darker of its tones taking precedence. Mysterious shadows danced around the tent, dull and terrifying from the woefully underpowered flashlight inside. The cries in the distance grew now to a background choir of tortured screams ringing in the heads of both Victor and Nancy. Some begged for help, some for mercy, all for respite.

"Nancy, what the fuck is this?" Victor whispered exasperatedly. The two clutched one another around the torso, knuckles white.

"Why is he doing this?" Nancy asked back, tears falling down her cheeks. She glanced at the shadows dancing on the tent walls, now screaming, "Why are you doing this?!?"

The screams halted.

Silence.

Then the voice, full of lingering black and noisome rot.

"When a tree falls in the woods and there's no one around to hear it, does it make a sound?"

Victor and Nancy, heartbeats raging, exchanged glances. Each face held the eyes of lost, demoralized children.

"Wh...wh...what?" Nancy whispered.

"You heard me. When a tree falls in the woods and there's no one around to hear it, does it make a sound?"

"Y...yes. Of course." Victor squeaked out.

A deep, rumbling cackle greeted the answer. The voice began again, its dark side presiding once more.

"Then how have I torn every pine around you out from the root without your hearing it?"

Nancy and Victor froze to their spot in the center of the tent, too scared to move, too scared to scream.

"So, the question remains..." The voice began again, now growling, "When I tear you both limb from limb and paint the woods red with your blood, will you hear each other scream?"

Victor shook violently, a howl of mortal fear rising in his lungs abruptly stopped at the threshold of his mouth, now agape. He stared into the eyes of his wife, eyes staring back but not seeing him, eyes flooding with catatonic insanity. The weight of the black evil surrounding them seemed to crush the air inside the tent.

A light, long scratching sound behind Nancy triggered a reflex reaction in her now silent body, and she turned to face it. She saw the imprint of a gnarled set of hands pressed against the tent wall from the outside. Long claws pushed into the nylon with almost enough forced to tear it. More and more gnarled hands appeared, picking and prodding the walls as choirs of agony screeched in the night outside.

"You will die before light!" the dark growling voice yelled. "You will die before the light!" it came again, now higher. The phrase repeated over and over, overlapping in every tone and cadence imaginable. All sense, logic, and reason fled both Nancy and Victor's heads, their previous life dispositions a hopeless, reckless lie. Warm trickles of urine flowed from Nancy, uncontrolled. She screamed until her voice gave out, her calls drowned out in insane music of the night. The sounds drilled into Victor's mind, now a pitch-black wall of dizzying idiot despair.

The gnarled handprints struck the tent floor, tossing unaware Nancy to the side and triggering Victor's innate basic instinct to run. He scrambled to his feet, slipping on the vomit he spewed not three minutes earlier, then launched himself at the tent door. Victor yanked the zipper down in a heaving, jerking motion and threw himself outside. Absurdly loud whooshes battered the tent as if massive wings beat furiously in the night air, and Victor's strained and gargling screams echoed everywhere. Even in Nancy's absent mind, the chorus of breaking bones and ripping flesh was unmistakable.

Nancy rolled on her side and stared up at the ceiling of the tent as large chunks of matter she could not see clearly struck it and thudded on the ground outside. A stream of thick, dark liquid flowed from above, dripping down the tent walls as Nancy rolled and wailed inside.

"Come outside, Nancy." The fetid voices called. "We're all waiting for you!"

The dark liquid pouring over the walls outside leaked through the open tent door and Nancy could see now that it was blood, filled with chunks of what she could only assume was human flesh. It pooled in a thick, rancid puddle by the open door and Nancy gagged, her head spinning.

Her vision grew spotty and darkened.

***

When Nancy Galloway opened her eyes, sunlight had drifted in through the tent door. She breathed in sudden, panicked breaths and glanced all around her. Her clothes were stained in brownish-red streaks, as was the rest of the tent inside.

"V-v-v-Victor?" She called out quietly. The tent door fluttered slightly from a breeze outside. Birds chirped from above and the sounds of children playing carried in from the distance.

"Victor!" Nancy cried again, hoarsely and scared. She sat in silence and shivered in the empty tent for five minutes.

Whimpering, Nancy edged her way to the tent door, her heart beating so fast and loud that it muted everything outside.

One…she told herself.

Two…

THREE.

Nancy shoved her head outside the tent. To her right stood the path she and her husband had walked the day before. To her left, roughly four hundred feet down the path, stood Green Valley Campgrounds, crowded with families. Nancy exited the tent, bewildered at the sight. She spun around in circles, growing dizzy quickly and feeling faint. Nancy knelt down and placed her head between her knees, attempting to regain her thoughts. Instead, she threw up.

***

Victor Galloway was never seen again. Nancy spent four years under the psychiatric care of a Dr. Kelly Remarr at the Sturgan Center for Women, a mental rehabilitation clinic in New Hampshire. Prosecutors initially believed that she had murdered her husband, but aside from the dried blood-drenched on her person and inside the tent, no physical evidence of murder surfaced. Her memory of the camping trip grew hazier with each passing day, though sometimes, and always in dreams, she could hear Victor's voice calling out to her, beckoning her to join the symphony of the night.

The End.

Kevin Buchholz is a filmmaker and TV producer in addition to his short story works. His first feature film project, "The Devil's Daughters", is currently in pre-production. He lives in Miami, Florida, and has an affinity for motorbikes, horror films, and FSU football.

Before and When My Teeth Came In by Erik Schechter

I always dreamed of having a daughter.

Penny.

I would've called her Penny. Penny is a good name. It belongs to a bold, little girl in dirty socks.

That's how I always imagined my daughter: wild, *free*. Chasing after squirrels in Central Park. Cooing at the warblers in the trees. Cutting stars out of yellow construction paper.

A little too idyllic, I know.

There would have been the terrible twos, then the sulky teens—black nail polish, fights and curfews, a barrage of *Ihateyou-Ihateyou-Ihateyou*. But I could've handled it.

Not that it matters anymore. I couldn't possibly have children with him.

***

"It's delicious."

That was me—before the bruises. I was lying, of course. The stew wasn't delicious. Far from it. It was salty and gelatinous, and it sloshed in my mouth like a dying eel.

My nostrils wrinkled at the smell.

But I forced it down anyway. Washed away the taste with a sip of merlot. Repeated the process with each spoonful until the bowl was half-gone.

Would you have eaten it? Maybe not.

But it was the dish of his people, and he made it for me, and I was in love with him. Had you seen that soft, expectant look in his eyes, you would've at least understood why I did it.

"Please stay the night," he finally said, satisfied that I had eaten enough.

"You'll have to read me another poem first," I said, setting my terms—*asserting myself*, but gently, with a playful lilt. "So who is it going to be? Ginsburg? Angelou?"

He just smiled at that and pulled me to his lips.

I spent the night at his apartment in Bay Ridge, atop a Yemeni bodega that sold loosies to Russian teens, so far south and west that it was just a few blocks from the piers.

He had this preposterously narrow bed wedged in between two bookcases, but we made it work. We wrestled on that thin plank of a mattress, giggled under the sheets. And afterward, I nuzzled against his sleek, pearl-colored body and dreamed of boats along the waterfront.

***

I remember waking up early in the morning to the screams of seagulls.

He was already in the bathroom, taking one of his interminable showers. He'd indulge in two, or even three, in a day. *It was one of his quirks,* I told myself, *that's all.*

***

When we first met, I thought him shy.

He just stood there in the corner, next to my *Urban/scape No.5,* clutching a leather-bound journal. He was so quiet, so inhumanly still. You could've mistaken him for a wax sculpture.

There had been a lot of new faces in the gallery that evening; I only noticed him once the crowd began to thin out. He gave me a faint smile— always the smile! —before turning back to the ceiling-high watercolor.

"Who's the guy?" I nudged a friend who was also showcasing a few pieces.

"Some poet, I think. Eastern European? Definitely foreign," he said, then adding with a hint of conspiracy, "I think he wants to talk to you."

"So why doesn't he just come over?"

"Who knows? Let's go to him."

"No, wait—!"

109

And, like that, my poet and I were introduced, and we stood together in front of *Urban/scape No.5*.

"It feels alive. I can see it swimming with tail and teeth and fins," he said. "How did you know when it was done?"

I always found the way he phrased things cryptic, as if he didn't just write in verse, but spoke it. Yet, despite that strangeness, there was something so endearing about how he asked about my painting and, more, how he waited through the explanation.

We would date for ten months, two weeks and three days.

***

"You need to eat," he said, leaning over my hospital bed with a Tupperware container and plastic spoon.

"I told you already. I don't want the stew." My head lolled back, and the room did laps around me. It felt like the time I went deep sea fishing with my dad and I puked all over the bow of the ship.

"Your body needs to rebuild," he insisted as if talking to a child. "It needs to recognize itself. The stew *will* help."

It was my first bout with the bruises.

We had been seeing each other for three months when, suddenly, in the span of a week, a dozen plum-colored splotches had spread across both my legs. I didn't think much about it when there was just one or two. But soon enough, I was researching exotic blood disorders online, working myself deeper and deeper into a panic with each page click.

My doctor didn't know what to make of it. She said it could be as simple as a vitamin deficiency and scheduled me for a blood test.

But when I came down with a fever, I was told to go to the emergency room.

"I know what you're thinking. It's not Ebola," my foreign poet snorted.

"How would you know?"

"Because I'm the most brilliant thing you've met," he said with a smile.

Maybe he expected me to laugh, but I didn't, so he took a more serious tone: "Think about it. You've never been to West Africa. You don't work in a hospital. All they're doing is checking off boxes."

His towering conceit annoyed me, but I was relieved all the same. So I ate his stew. This time, the whole bowl slithered down my throat.

***

For the week I was in the hospital, he visited every day, stationing himself in the vinyl-covered chair by my side. He seemed worn out at times and would retreat deep within his own inscrutable thoughts, leaving behind a cold husk of a body.

Other times, though, he was all fire and frenzy, weaving epics tales of sunken galleons and ageless sea creatures so detailed, so well-crafted, that I'd find myself transported from my hospital bed to another realm.

I never knew when he'd turn manic or hide within himself. But he always came armed with treats. He had this canvas bag from which he'd produce dark chocolate, sour candies, and vitamin water.

"Dark chocolate improves vascular function," he said, stroking my ear.

The nurses gave him the side-eye when he said things like that. They also didn't like how he studied my medical chart or touched their machines or questioned every little procedure.

The doctors tried talking above him, around him, anything but face him dead-on. It was visceral with them—like they had met a walking, thinking virus and all they wanted to do was jab it with a syringe.

"So, tell me. Did *you* graduate from medical school?" an irritated resident asked him.

"Did you?" my poet hissed back.

When a doctor or nurse would leave the room, he'd curl his lip and declare said person a "little shopkeeper." That was his term for anyone he thought an idiot: little shopkeeper.

I'm not sure if it was an idiom translated from another language or one of his own poetic invention, but he called many people "little shopkeepers." It could be intimidating.

But he never refused a request of mine. Not once.

***

Russians thought he might be Ukrainian. The Ukrainians said he was Polish. Others swore they heard hints of a Macedonian accent. He laughed at all this and announced that he was from Belarus, that he had been born in the mud of the Dnieper River.

"More poetry," I told people.

He didn't have any friends, and he never talked much about family. "My parents died when I was a baby, and I have no brothers or sisters," he'd repeat with mechanical precision, and though the idea of a baby raising itself was absurd, I never pressed him.

He'd tell me the truth when he was ready, I had decided.

Anyway, there was no point in exhausting energy on it. He already consumed enough.

I remember this gallery party after my release from the hospital. All the guests at the table had lifted their champagne flutes for a toast, but he just stared off in the distance, his face taking on an unsettlingly alien cast, as if the muscles in his cheeks had melted away.

I begged him to participate, to be normal for me, just this once. "Please don't make me defend you again," I whispered, hearing my own voice clog with tears.

***

When summer rolled around, we didn't see much of each other during the day. He'd sequester himself in his Bay Ridge apartment, writing poems about seashells and starfish, while I'd work in my studio or meet up with friends who avoided his company.

Then, one afternoon, he dropped by the studio. He was wearing sunglasses and a cowboy hat and said that he just returned from an overnighter in the country. There was a lake near the cabin where he'd stayed, and he had gone skinny dipping at night...

"Are those umbrellas?" I asked, motioning to the long packages under his arms.

"Parasols. One for me and one for you," he smiled, holding them out like batons.

"Um, that's ridiculous," I laughed.

"Well, I think they're stylish and practical," he said, opening his and posing like a *GQ* model under its lace hems. "Henceforth, this will be my regular summertime accoutrement!"

See? That was the insane, brilliant creature who made me forget his other side.

As I snapped pictures of him with my smartphone, he asked if I wanted to go with him to an outdoor Asian market in Queens. They had some truly strange fruit there, he said.

"You mean now?" I asked, considering my canvas.

"Come on, it'll be fun! I still have the rented car," he said.

***

"We will always be together," he told me one September night as we strolled along a stretch of dock jutting out into the Hudson.

I paused and sucked in the briny air of the estuary.

Those five words: *We will always be together*—I took them for the rarest declaration of love. They were the long-awaited sign

113

that I had cracked his stony carapace, that he would finally let me in, and I would be so very gentle with his secret wounds.

As we looked at the glittering waves, I rubbed my arms: The bruises had come back. But what did it matter? I'd just have some stew, and they'd fade in a day or two. They barely ached, anyway.

I suppose it could have waited, but at that moment, everything was so perfect. "What do you think of the name Penny?" I asked him.

***

The following week, my doctor wanted to schedule yet another follow-up blood test.

"Why?" I asked. "Is there something wrong with the one I just did?"

"The lab got some nonsense results," she said. "Probably a sample contamination issue. It's nothing to worry about."

"Oh, Ok." My fingertips already started to feel numb.

"I did have a question, though. Do you happen to work around radioactive particles or some place that stocks genetic samples from animals?"

When I got off the phone, my poet shook his head and muttered, "Such a little shopkeeper."

"You mean the doctor?" I asked.

He just smirked.

***

"You're being absurd," he said, wincing at the sunlight streaming in from the window. "The bruises are all in your head. I can see that now. And those doctors, they are poor disciples of Asclepius. It's all just big dollars to them."

I put down the coffee and stared at him. Then the words burst out like a geyser: "You think I'm being a hypochondriac!? That

114

this is psychosomatic? I don't know what your problem is with Western medicine. But you can keep your stews and all-natural remedies. If I want to have a blood test or see a specialist, I will. Got it?"

"Listen, I didn't mean—," he started.

"—No, you stay right fucking here," I growled, scooping up my handbag and storming out of the café and then down the street.

Texts and calls followed; I ignored them all. For six days in a row, he sent roses to my studio, all with very contrite notes. There was this one haiku that was so beautiful I had to take it home and press it between the pages of my sketchbook:

Send ships of purple,
And station men at Sidon.
Does her heart sail back?

Finally, on the seventh day, I relented.

"I miss you too…" I mumbled over the phone. "OK, we'll do dinner…Tomorrow night." I didn't tell him that I had already redone the blood test and was awaiting the results.

The following night I was ready to cancel on the poet. Tiny bruises had begun to spot my abdomen, and I felt a touch warm. But he showed up early in a rented SUV with tinted windows.

He smiled broadly as he exited the massive, off-road vehicle and jogged around the front to open the passenger side door. Despite my incipient foul mood, I found myself tittering as he invited me into the SUV with a little, valet-like bow and sweep of the hand.

"So, do you like it?" he asked.

Those were the last words I heard before waking up chained to a wall.

***

I blamed myself.

There had been so many clues: the incessant showers, that stupid parasol, his missing childhood, the inhuman stillness and all the rest. I could've pieced them together. Really, I could have. Instead, I made excuses because it was easier than believing the impossible.

That's how you end up in a dark cellar with a monster.

The basement smelled of mildew and pinecones. What little light there was leaked through the seams of a weathered bulkhead door at the top of the staircase. I could see that the cellar walls were lined with brown brick—old, uneven, some even cracked.

Once upon a time, the cellar might have stored chopped wood.

Not anymore, though.

The shackle biting my ankle was padlocked and linked to a long chain that wove through an O-ring set in the wall. The Poet had already placed a bowl of stew on the floor in front of me and was pointing to a white, ten-gallon bucket in the corner.

"For your needs," he said.

"Why are you doing this to me?" I was having trouble even forming the words.

"Because you're very special," he said, pressing his hands together and shaking them at me. "I've invested so much in you. I couldn't lose you to a hospital now."

"You know, people will be looking for me," I choked.

"Think so? You don't have a regular job, and I've updated your Facebook page," he said, pulling out his smartphone, "Hold on, you'll be so impressed. I got your voice just right. '*FB Honies: I'm working on a new project. Huge opportunity. Crazy new deadline. I'll be up for air in a month. #MIA4art.*'"

"And after the month?" I asked, feeling my stomach turn to water.

"You'll see," he answered.

***

My body locked up whenever he would creep down the cellar stairs. His limbs moved in horrible—impossible—directions. *Like tentacles. They wriggled and stretched like tentacles.* His skin too, it was off. Without cologne, it smelled faintly like raw salmon.

He was no longer hiding from the little shopkeepers.

Isn't this what you wanted? I thought. *To see his secret self?*

Every morning, he'd show up with a garden hose and canvas bag. He'd hand me a thin hotel bar of soap and spray me with the hose as I scrubbed. Afterward, he'd inspect my skin and pull on my gums, refill my food bowl, and empty my bucket.

He did it with a smile as if it were all a joke.

Sometimes, he'd even pat my head before slinking back upstairs.

"Good girl," he'd say.

He didn't seem the least bit surprised when my black curls began falling out. By the end of the first week, I was rocking back and forth, arms around my folded legs, wailing over fistfuls of hair, and all he could say was "It'll get better soon."

The bruises, though, never returned, and at first I took it as a welcome sign.

But I felt my skin changing. It was getting thin, like those cheap plastic bags you get with your groceries, and the color was fading too—my natural golden brown turning a sickly gray. A rotting corpse gray.

I knew the stew was making me sick. But there was nothing else to eat in the cellar— except for the occasional millipede and pillbug. And for the first three days, I didn't touch them.

But you do funny things when you think you're about to die.

I ate bugs.

I prayed to God too. Negotiated, actually. There, in the dark, on a carpet of dirt.

"Please, Jesus, save me," I whispered, my fingers woven together. "Save me, and I will be a better person. Give me a chance to live a less selfish life."

The insects provided an extra bit of nutrition. Jesus sent me JFK.

It was an old Kennedy half-dollar. I found the coin while scouring the floor for millipedes. It'd take time, and I'd have to be subtle, but I figured that I could use the half-dollar to chip away at the grainy mortar holding one of those cracked bricks in the wall.

***

The blood—deep garnet in color and inky to the touch—pooled around his head.

The air above it smelled metallic.

It probably never occurred to him that he could make a mistake; he had managed everything so well until then. But as soon as he stepped within range, I hit him fast—hit him *hard*, two quick blows: one, two. And down he went.

His foot twitched for a second before his body went perfectly still. But even as he lay there on the cellar floor, face-up, eyes closed, my hands vibrated with fear and adrenaline. Far from injured, the Poet looked as if he were dreaming on a red satin napkin.

Can creatures like him even die this way? This could be another trick.

In the stories, there was always a ritual or a special weapon. Hercules had to kill his giant on foreign soil. Fire and a golden sword did in the Hydra of Lerna. Poor Lucy required a stake through the heart and a mouth packed with garlic.

No one ever talks about half a brick to the back of the head.

I kicked his ribs—he didn't flinch. So with a quiet prayer in my throat, I knelt over his body and struck him again, this time in the temple. Had I the strength, I would have shattered all the bones in his face. But three weeks in the cellar had left me dazed and exhausted: a listless, ashen thing in the gloom.

I fished through his pockets for the key to my leg shackles. I had hoped to find his smartphone too. With any luck, it would have some juice, and I would call the police, and they would come to my rescue sirens blaring, just like they do on TV.

I found the key, his wallet and a plastic key fob to a rented car. But there was no phone.

***

I made my escape anyway.

***

The sunlight stabbed my corneas as I cleared the cellar doors.

Instinctively, I spun around, out of the furnace-glare, and faced the old cabin that squatted atop my make-shift dungeon. The narrow window panes were covered with plywood and tarp, and the pockmarked roof looked like it had seen better days.

Twice I circled the cabin looking for his rented SUV, but the vehicle wasn't there. Nor was there any gravel trail that could support a car.

The clearing where the cabin stood was hemmed in by a green-gray wall of spruce that bristled in the wind. There had to be a road hidden behind the trees, I figured. But where? I pointed the key fob north, west, south, and east. There was no telltale beep.

The heat, meanwhile, was driving me mad. It was autumn: even in a wool jacket, I should've been shivering—it didn't make any sense. Then, a single, horrible word struck me: *parasol*. The fall weather was perfectly normal. *I* was one who was the broiling. He hadn't just poisoned my skin. *He had made me like him*.

I gritted my teeth. *The doctors will fix me*, I repeated to myself. *They can do anything these days.* All I had to do was get off this sweltering hilltop.

119

But how?

By thinking like a monster.

I sniffed at the air. The incense of pinecones mingled with the musk of dead, orange leaves. Beyond that, I could smell the fur of squirrels in the trees, the dust coming off the wings of passing birds—and the Poet's own fishiness left on the grass.

This new kaleidoscope of scents was almost too much to take. Still, I honed in on his smell and trailed it through the woods.

***

Under the glare of the sun, my skin began to burn and itch. The trees provided some cover as I walked, but not enough. Often, I'd have to crouch in the shade until I could summon the strength to continue onward.

That was when I noticed the changes in my hand.

The skin, and muscles underneath, had faded into a jellyfish-like translucence.

Waves of nausea swept over me. *This can't be real. No! This must be heatstroke.* Still, I couldn't stop looking at my hands—at my wrists and arms. The bones and veins flashed garishly through a fog of tissue. Soon I was touching my cheeks. *Was it my face too?*

I followed his trail for as long as I could. The sun was ravaging my body, and the longer I walked, the worse it got. My lungs felt like broken pieces of flint. Flashes of orange exploded in the corners of my eyes.

More than a doctor, I desperately wanted a river. A whole river to bathe in.

***

By late afternoon, he found me hiding under the bough of a spruce tree. My skin had already started to crack and ooze, and I

120

was pressing my naked body against the cool, black soil around the trunk.

"Oh, God. Please…," I croaked, seeing him at the foot of the tree.

"Please, what?" he asked. He was smiling despite the gash to his forehead.

"Leave me *alone!*"

"Alone to do what?" he chuckled. "Go back to East Harlem? Paint? Eat pizza? You wouldn't last two weeks there. They'd find what was left of you clogging the bathtub drain."

"What did you do to me?"

"I took your life away," he nodded somberly. "But I can give you a new one, a better one. I can give you all the rivers and seas, all the oceans of this world."

"How?" I asked.

"By getting out from under that tree and coming with me."

"You think you won, don't you?" I spat out. "You think you own me now. But"—I looked at my wraith-like hands—"what if I just kill myself?"

The Poet paused for a moment to consider my threat.

"Well, you could probably do it tonight—or in two months from now, or in five years," he answered in his casual Bay Ridge apartment tone. "So why not see the world first?"

I thought about my imaginary daughter.

Penny would've fought the monster. Again and again and again. She would've kicked his hands away. Lunged at his eyes like an alley cat. I just know it.

That's what wild little girls in dirty socks do.

I could see Penny slipping around him, scrambling out from under the tree and up the next hill. Maybe there'd be a town on the other side. Maybe not. Either way, she would have run as far as her burning lungs could take her.

And she would've died just the same.

"Why does your skin look like that?" I asked. His face and hands were sunburned, but otherwise, they were normal. Human.

It wasn't fair.

***

Every story must begin somewhere. Mine, I suppose, starts along the Hudson. It's dusk now. The winter tide is lapping at my thighs.

I look out at the scaly waves in the distance. He is but a bobbing head.

We were here before, only a few months ago, up there on the docks. Just a painter and her poet strolling in the night. He had told me that we would always be together, and I thought that he was, in his own closed-off way, finally surrendering to passion.

But, no, he was just stating a fact: Manhattan is an island; sturgeon is a fish; I would always be with him—facts.

He had already begun the process of molding me, of remaking me into something more compatible with himself, something sleek and hairless, with new lungs and a new skin.

And new *teeth*.

Oh, yes, they came in last week, long and jagged.

Under his ministrations, I witnessed myself transform into a living display case of bone, viscera, and arteries. But, really, what's that compared to growing a mouth full of angled razors? Of slicing one's face when speaking?

Do you know how many words we form with our lips?

I think about my dagger teeth. It would be so easy to gnaw at my wrists, open up veins and finish this thing, right here, right now, in full view of New York's glittering towers. But I suppose there will always be time for suicide—or murder, if I choose.

The Hudson's burbling water is cold on my glassy skin. The depths will be colder still. He promises to show me wrecked galleons and ageless sea creatures. We will have adventures little shopkeepers could only dream of.

All I have to do is *sink*.

The End.

Erik Schechter

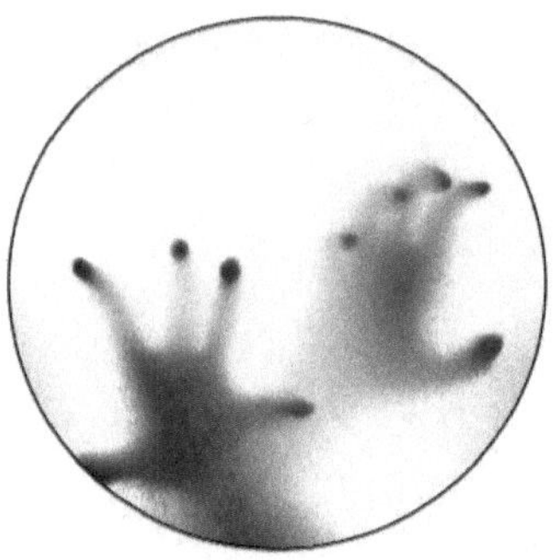

Details not released at this time

Foil by F. Pierce Skinner

All these fuckin things everywhere. Tinfoil all bent and crinkled in the shapes of people bout the size of my hand, all over the shelves that run long the wall cross from the window. Been makin em since he was six. We ain't had money for no goddamn toys, not all his life, specially not now since Edna left and the government's fuckin with my ebt again, cut me down to one-sixty-eight a month, like I can do anythin' with that. All these fuckin things everywhere. Tin foil people. A poor Florida boy's toys. You'd think by fifteen heeda grown out of it. He just keeps it up to spite me, I know it. His window is open. Air is thick like August air but it ain't even June yet.

I check my watch. It's past 'leven. Soon as he crawls through that window, I'ma beat him. You can't go through life thinkin you're smarter'n everyone. That's how you get your ass beat. That's the shit'll get you killed. Don't know what he's sneaking out for. Sure as shit ain't got no girl. Might be drugs. Might just be to piss me off. We haven't gotten along since his mama left. I told her all I needed was more time. I told her I'd get help. I can't help being angry. Can't help what I do. I ain't made myself. But women don't give a shit. Women got no patience. All a woman wants is an excuse to cause trouble. And I guess women ain't made 'emselves either but still, fuck em.

Don't know what time it is when I get sick of waitin and I'm too drunk to remember most of what happens. I know I rip the shelves off the wall. The little foil men all over. A lot of them broken, all torn up. Little shiny shits all over the brown carpet. The ones that ain't broke or torn up laying there all stiff like dead bugs.

And then I leave the room. Think I shut the window, lock it, check the doors. He ain't gettin back in here. Not tonight.

I remember staring at the stain on the ceiling in my bedroom, the one that looks like a nipple, and then blackness.

***

Somethin wakes me. Like a plane gone over the house, 'cept ain't no airports 'round here. I slide off the bed. I stand up. A voice, bursting out of the darkness down the hall, comin from the kitchen.

"He's awake," it says, full and wide and loud as God, not even tryin to be quiet.

Someone's in my fuckin house.

I run to the closet. Heart's a ball peen hammer against my ribs. I don't even bother yankin on the light, just reach up onto the shelf for the gun case, but it's not there. I reach up and pull the string and the light comes on and there, on the floor, is the gun case. It's open. And empty.

Voice says, "Come into the kitchen. We need to talk."

I back out of the closet slow. Can't stop lookin at the empty case. Blood's thick and movin too fast through me and it's making me dizzy. Someone's in my house. They got my gun.

My boy…

I say "Peyton," out loud, and then I'm running down the hall to my boy's room. Door's open. Light's on, how I left it. He still ain't there. Somethin bad's happenin, I know that now. My boy's gone and there's someone in my kitchen with my gun. I follow the voice, toward the dark kitchen, into it, the only light's the light from microwave clock. I flip on the light.

Ain't no one there.

Kitchen's empty.

Then I see it.

Two o' them little tin foil people, right there on the counter. One of 'em sits in front of the microwave, bigger'n the other one, made out of a lot of bunched up foil that makes it look fat around the middle, legs crossed, lookin like somethin religious, like a little tin foil Buddha.

Then, a sound. Somethin movin cross the linoleum. I spin round, but the whiskey ain't through with me and I'm already dizzy somethin awful and I almost fall down but I catch myself on the 'fridgerator door handle and pull myself up straight. The scuttlin sound again, behind me on the counter. I turn slow this time.

The tin foil people ain't in the same places. The big one what in front of the microwave, the Buddha-lookin one, now it's standin on the edge of the counter, near the sink. Like it *stood up* while I wasn't lookin'.

A low moan gurgles from somewhere deep in me that's startin to understand. I breathe deep and heavy and the air feels like sand in my throat and in my chest. This is a moment, I know, when life stops followin the rules. Things're different, now, and I know it the same way I know I'm livin without nobody tellin me. This is one of them things that happens, every now and again, when the world turns into somethin else, like when the Lord was born.

"Ron. Stop fucking around," the voice says. The voice is comin from the foil man near the sink. Don't make no sense but it don't have to. Things're different, now.

I look down at the foil man. The big one by the sink. The Buddha. It lifts its head up at me.

"Ronald Boggs," it says, "father of Peyton Boggs."

"Y'all..." I start. My voice is a wisp, drowned out neath the sand and the heartbeats all fightin for space in my throat. "Y'all really alive, huh?" I swallow. "This really happenin?"

"Yes," another voice says. This one belongs to a foil man with a torn off piece of wallpaper as a cape, stuck at the front by a twisted-up paperclip. It's also holdin my .38 Special with both of its arms. One of 'em's wrapped around the trigger. Barrel's pointed at my belly button.

I swallow.

"So...so...so this is it, huh? This is when y'all...y'all kill me? For the drinkin? For being a bad father? For beatin my son? For breaking his...his toys'n...doin all that? This's where y'all kill me?"

They don't say nothin.

"Y'all some kinda...some kinda...manifestation, ain'tcha? Some kinda...divine retribution shit, huh?"

They still don't say nothin'. Just standin there on the counter.

Little foil men and one of 'em's got my gun and my boy is missin.

Oh, Lord, Lord, my boy is *missin'*.

A sound like a sigh comes from the Buddha. "Ron," it says. If I squint, I can see its little tin foil mouth move. Standing still, I can see little grooves like eyes and cheekbones and nostrils. The nostrils flare. Tiny little tin foil nostrils pullin air into tiny tin foil lungs.

"Y'all...are really alive..."

The one holding the gun hooks its arm around the trigger. "We're going for a drive," it says.

***

They make me put the bolt cutters from my old repo job in the truck bed before we leave.

The foil man with the gun stands on the passenger seat, keeping the gun barrel level with my liver. The Buddha's on the dashboard, steadyin itself against the windshield, tellin me where to go. A third one--a woman, I guess, since this one's got little tin foil tits--sits next to the gearshift holdin my fishin knife. I don't know where I am. They done taken me off 5th onto the highway, off onto the Okeechobee Scenic. Passed St. Mary's a ways back and now there ain't nothin. Just the busted up road giving my tires hell and the dark all around and the smell of brackish water and swamp rot and the humidity beadin on my forehead and down my chest and back.

"Slow down," the Buddha says. I ease off the gas.

"Here," the Buddha says, "Turn right."

I bring the car to a stop and look where the little foil arm is pointin.

"Ain't no turn," I say.

"Turn. Right. Ron."

I look over't the passenger seat, at the gun. My gun.

"Sure..." I swallow, wipe sweat out of my eyes. "Relax. Ain't no road there, 'sall I'm sayin'. I lived here all my life, I'm just tellin you ain't no road."

I turn right, off of the road, cross mud and grass that I can feel the tires start to sink into. Outside, I can hear the croaking of baby gators.

"Keep straight," the Buddha says.

"Please..." I say, "Please tell me where we're going."

They don't say nothin. I just keep drivin into the swamp.

Straight ahead, just past the treelike, a dark squat hunk of blackness that's darker than the surrounding night.

"Stop here."

I stop.

"Get out of the car," the Buddha says. "Get the bolt cutters out of the back."

"Please," I say, "Guys, please."

They don't say nothin'. I start to cry again.

"Get out of the car--"

"Please--"

"And get the bolt cutters--"

I can change, fellas--"

"--out of the back."

"Please. I can change. I can be a better father--"

"Ron," the Gunman says, "We're not going to kill you."

I'm able to force the tears to stop for long enough to turn and look down at the foil man with the gun.

"What I mean to say is," it shrugs, "We don't *want* to *have* to kill you."

"We probably won't have to kill you," the Buddha says.

The Gunman says, "We have faith in you."

"Why...why's this happenin'?"

"If we tell you," the Buddha says, "You won't believe us."

"Won't believe what?"

"Get the bolt cutters, Ron."

It's useless. I start to cry again.

I get out of the car. I get the bolt cutters.

***

The Woman has the flashlight and the Gunman is behind me. The Buddha's holdin my fishin knife walking next to her.

They lead me to a squat, rotted, graffitied trailer in the middle of the swamp. Fuckin' ancient thing, all sagged in the middle like a sick horse. Flashlight shines on the door, which is crooked and held shut by a bike lock. Looks new. Shiny black. Says *Krypton* on the side.

"Cut it," the Buddha says, and points to the lock.

I stumble forward, tired enough, now, from the terror and the cryin, that I figure I might as well do what they say and get this whole fuckin' thing over with.

I cut it. The pieces fall into the mud. The door swings open.

The smell of swamp-rot and mold and dead animals. Snake shit. A million little invisible things, all dyin at once. I cough and cover my mouth and back away but something stabs me in the ankle. I look down at the foil figures, all standin in a line behind me, the swamp-dulled moonlight slipping off their foil crinkle bodies like dirty white sludge. The gun is pointed at my knees. The Buddha holds the fishing knife against my ankle.

"I ain't a bad father," I say.

"Jesus, Ron," says the Gunman, "You're so fucking pathetic." The Buddha says, "He's almost here."

"Who?" I squint into the flashlight as one of them raises it directly into my eyes. "Who's almost here?"

"Go!" they all bark in unison.

"Fuck you!"

I think real hard about bringing the bolt cutters up over my head, slammin it down, crushin' their tiny little tin foil bodies.

But then I look at the gun again. No. This ain't where I wanna die. Sure as shit ain't *how*, neither.

I turn and walk into the trailer. They follow me.

Everything's soggy and covered in mud and mold. The flashlight falls on the floor, showin' me that there's footprints in the mud. I follow them into the trailer, to a tiny kitchen table. The flashlight beam lifts to show me three hard Igloo coolers sittin there on the table. These don't look so old, either. And they got chains wrapped 'round 'em tight, with big thick locks on 'em. The smell is big and brown and awful and I lift arm and breathe into the crook of my elbow, which smells like sweat and whiskey.

The Buddha has climbed up onto the table, and he's standin in the flashlight beam next to the red cooler in the middle.

He taps it with his knife.

"Cut it," he says.

"Okay," I say.

The Buddha steps aside.

I lower my arm, bring up the bolt cutters, and somehow I know that whatever happens in the next few seconds is gonna change all the seconds after that till the end of time and for this reason it seems like time moves slow, real slow, like the world knows it's about to die and it just wants to hold on for just a little longer.

I cut the chain.

The cooler lid falls open.

The smell's of a sudden reckless, and it sure as shit ain't no swamp rot. I look down, into the cooler.

A face. Its eyes open and empty, all ate up by bugs and the wet air, its skin swollen and bruised. The mouth is pulverized into a weird, toothless *O* kept that way by fish hooks and fishin' line wrapped around the back of the head.

But I know the face, still, even all dead and half-rotted up like that, I know it. I know it's my Edna. Edna, who done run out on me last month. Just left one day, never came back. My wife's there, in the igloo cooler, all dead and half-rotted up and that's just too much for me to take. I throw up, right there onto the kitchen table. I back away until I hit the wall.

I shut my eyes but my wife's broken face is there when I do so I open them again. I wish someone would explain what's goin on. I wish none of this was happenin. I wish that so goddamn *bad*.

"Look!" Little sharp foil hands, strong like a man's, grab my face, twist it to look into the eyeless ball of foil that is the Buddha's face, like I'm supposed to see somethin in it. It says, "*He*. Did This."

"What...what..."

"She was his first."

"What...what are you...?" I try to move my head but the little foil man won't let me. It squeezes. My skull feels bout to crack.

The little foil man moves my face, forces it, slowly, to a patch of dirt in the opposite corner. The flashlight moves to show me another twig and another white ribbon.

"A baby, Ron. A baby he took out of an unlocked car in front of The Circle K on 3rd Street. That was his second."

I blink. The grip relaxes. My breath steadies. A long time passes. It hits me durin the silence, Edna ain't leave me. She ain't give up on me. She ain't run off. She been here. Dead, but she ain't leave me. Somebody killed her. The relief this gives me is so big and wide and pure, like a big black mountain got picked up off my soul and I can almost think clearly 'cause of it.

"What...what do you...want from me?" I ask.

"Your son," the Buddha says. "Your son did this."

The black mountain falls back down.

"My...my...You mean...Peyton?"

Flashlight sweeps across the clay, lands in my face. I squint into it.

"Peyton did this?"

And, just like I know I'm alive, just like I know this is all really happenin, I know what they sayin' is true. Same way I know the Lord was born and my momma's name, may she rest in peace.

"We're giving you a choice, Ron," says the Gunman, steppin into the beam of the flashlight, sets the gun down gently onto the table beside my vomit drippin off the table.

Understanding hits like heartburn, pulls it all up to the top.

"You want me to kill...kill my *son*?"

They're all silent for another few heartbeats.

"Calm down, Abraham," the one with the wallpaper cape says, sarcastic like. "You don't love him. You know it, *we* sure as shit know it. And he's a blight upon the world, so...." it drags out the last word, shrugs.

"He's...he's my son..."

"He's a blight, Ron. A *thing*. Only way something like him could get through was to be born. Don't make him human any more than me."

"Look," the Buddha says, "You have to see how this is at least partially your fault."

"I can't...I can't kill my son..."

"He'll kill again. He won't ever, *ever* stop."

"He's...he's my son..." I shut my eyes, but there's Edna's face again. "Oh, God. Oh, Jesus." I start to sob but there's no tears left, just fear and confusion and agony that all swirl around in my chest and limbs like a hurricane. Like a category five. I take two steps toward the table, pick up the gun.

"He's here," the Buddha groans. The Woman turns off the flashlight. Oily black eats everything up. I feel the Woman lay the flashlight down across my feet. I hear them all back away into the dark. I bend down, pick up the flashlight.

The Buddha's voice from the dark says, "This is your chance."

The sound of a bicycle chain clackin nearer, tires rollin over the dead leaves and twigs. Footsteps squelch in the mud outside the trailer. Then they stop.

A long, long minute goes by in the dark before a figure, short and thin, appears in the doorway, a black human shape framed by purple midnight.

I turn on the flashlight.

My son freezes in the doorway. Dirty gray t-shirt and jean shorts. Eyes hidden under that heavy Irish brow he got from his momma. Thin brown hair that he got from me.

A plastic bag drops out of his arms, spills open onto the trailer floor. It's something wet and small and heavy. I don't look down. I *don't*.

"Peyton?"

He just stands there, doesn't know what to do, lifts his head a little, stares straight into the light. I can see it. His face. Under the skin of it, little veins like spider legs. His sweat is black, like oil runnin down his face and I know all of a sudden without a shadow of a doubt that if I shot him now he'd be full of nothin' but oil and spiders.

A long silence.

"Dad," he says, finally. He doesn't say anything else. "Peyton...what'd you do?"

My voice is shakin. A wave of nausea hits me and I get dizzy again and my shoulder pressed against the wall is the only reason I'm still standin up.

"Do it, Ron," the Buddha's voice hisses from the dark. Without bein able to see him, it sure does sound an awful lot like the voice of God. "Do it now."

"Thought this might happen someday" Peyton says. He looks around, calm as springtime, his eyes land on the bolt cutters like a fly on a turd. He kneels down slow, picks them up before I can really get a handle on what's happenin. "You will not deter my becoming."

"Peyton," I say, "Please."

Peyton slings 'em up over his shoulder and swings it like a baseball bat. The metal slams into the side of my head and then

I'm breathin the mud and dust on the floor. The darkness is colored white like a hot acid sky.

"Peyton..." I cough, roll over onto my back. The flashlight's on the floor under the table, the cone of light thrown toward the graffitied wall. I try to move but that just makes everythin hurt more so I stop. The side of my head is wet and I know I'm in a bad, bad way. I hear the little foil men moving across the floor in the darkness.

My son starts to scream.

I feel the gun slide out of my hand.

"No..." I groan, try to get a grip on the gun but it's too late. "We gave you a chance," the Buddha's voice is moving away, toward the screamin.

Smell of decay. Graffitied wall. Edna's deadness. Bike locks and chains and a big wide *O*. All just happened too fast. Eyes ain't closed but the dark comes on anyway.

Gun goes off with a big loud bang that I can feel like a slap across my whole body.

Screamin stops.

Somethin heavy hits the ground. I know it's my son. I know my boy is dead.

The little tin foil Buddha. He killed my son. Shot him dead with my .38 Special.

Ain't no sound, now.

Then, tiny footsteps.

I roll over, look up, and, would ya believe it, there's Edna, tall and strong, her clothes all dirty and wet and covered in black oil and crawling with tiny spiders and where her head should be there's a big thick ball of tin foil with no eyes and no nostrils and no cheekbones, nothin that says it's tryin to look human anymore, just a big ball with a wide mouth cut into it and when it opens to say, "We gave you a chance, Ron" I can see the blackness inside of it, and there are stars in it and the stars are shivering. The voice ain't Edna's. It's the Buddha's voice.

"That's more than most things get."

It bothers me how all of this is gonna look if anyone ever finds us. Like I shot my son in a trailer in the middle of the woods and he killed me with the bolt cutters and people will talk about it forever. They'll prolly reckon I killed Edna, too, and the dead baby that's still in the cooler. No one would ever think a kid done all this. But I knew that boy was no goddamn good. I knew it from the very start.

I close my eyes and the dark is thick like August air and full of baby spiders and their little legs feel just awful but I can't move. I won't ever move again. I'll just be here in the dark with the spiders crawlin on me forever and the itching feels awful, just awful.

Oh, I wish this wasn't happenin.

I wish that so goddamn *bad*.

The End.

F. Pierce Skinner

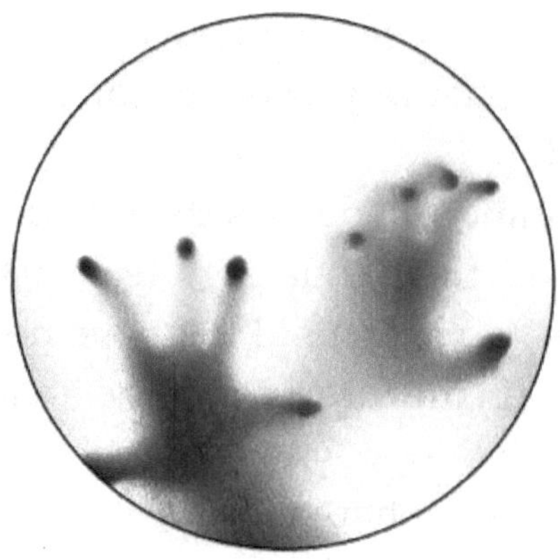

Details not released at this time

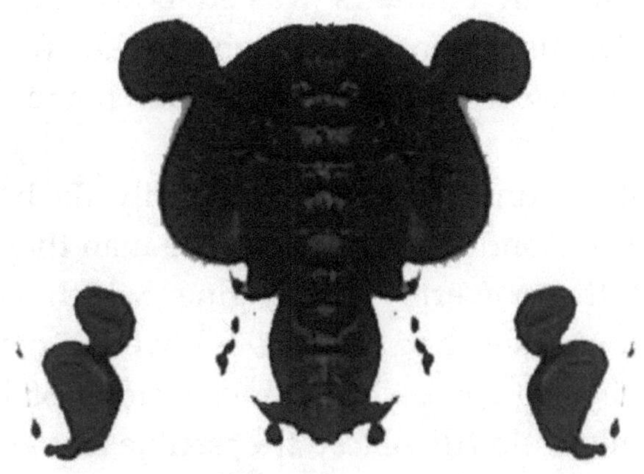

Dogs of Light by Mary Renzi

The window of his old bedroom gave Hunter Martin a clear view of the 1968 Ford Mustang parked across Myrtle Street; a For-Sale sign stickered to its windshield. His heart raced as he gazed down at it. The Mustang was the only thing that could still rouse adrenaline in Hunter's wasted body. He saw magical potential in the rust-eaten, once bright- yellow frame—a project that could transform him, that could make him *tougher*, somehow.

Gazing at it, Hunter forgot, momentarily, the heavy footsteps in the next room, and the tyranny of the man they belonged to. Thoughts of the powerful 428 engine, which Hunter would rebuild all shiny-new and perfect, allowed a nice amnesia to wash over him, so for a short time, visions of hemispherical pistons and mig welds displaced the terrible fear which ensnared him beneath the guardian's twisted rule.

Even the whole damn crucible of his past year at the Celerion Medical Compound washed away on the Mustang's powerful tide. Like how they had quarantined Hunter from sunlight. Like how the darkness only broke when Hunter *hallucinated* light.

He had a recurring vision in his pitch-black quarters of dogs that were made from light—a whole pack of lumbering canines with stilty legs who licked Hunter's face with firework tongues like Roman candles. He had named them: Sheriff, Buster, Beastie.

Real or not, the dogs helped Hunter survive Celerion. Their radiance kept him alive. He would have died from hopelessness there.

"This research will help our descendants become invulnerable to a spectrum of possible disasters," the scientists had assured him, pep-talking on his importance in their grand experiments. Grand experiments which would allow the human body to(among other things) produce vitamin D without sunlight, and to function on close to zero nutrients. In addition, the lab-coats reminded Hunter, he would be paid handsomely for his contribution. *Handsomely* meaning fifty grand for one year of Hunter's life.

Now back home, with the guardian's significant debts paid off, Hunter had three thousand dollars left to his name. He prayed it was enough for the Mustang as he listened through the thin bedroom walls. The guardian moved so heavily, like a giant. There was always that cavernous smell of wet earth and sulfur. Hunter's respite wouldn't be long, he knew.

He watched as two kids played stickball on the cracked asphalt in temperature-controlled UV suits, shooting figure eights around the Mustang and a broken-down jalopy. Even in their bulky suits, on the dead street, the kids looked so care-free.

***

With the sun safely set, Hunter could finally leave without donning his bulky Ulra-V suit. It was time to head outside for a look at the yellow beauty under moonlight. The thought of even being near the car soothed Hunter, and sent a clean buzz of joy throughout his tanked, lab-rat body. The car would be his. It *had* to be.

When he had asked New Wife that morning, hadn't she told him the vehicle had been gathering dust for months? The owner would probably take the first offer he gave. Hunter would start low.

Radio music eddied from the lightened living area as Hunter passed the archway. It felt inviting: the soft light, the music, the smell of food, but Hunter knew better.

He turned the front door-handle, when New Wife's smoke-slagged voice called him hoarsely back.

She stood at the kitchen-pass, beating flies from hunks of meat, throwing the large pieces into a bucket of marinade. Her skin had the same red sheen as it had in the hot afternoon. Salt crystals glistened in the dark hairs above her lip. She handed

Hunter his bowl of beef broth, which scorched his hand as it sloshed over the rim.

The guardian sat by the clock-radio in his favorite red armchair—*somehow able to sleep like that*—but he awoke as suddenly as a snoozing dragon, and appraised Hunter with feral eyes.

"Sit down with me," he ordered. Then softened his edict with, "You earned it, *son*."

The guardian's visage had frightened Hunter ever since he was a small boy: The wild, yellow sclera of his eyes, the iridescent shimmer of his hydrophobic skin, the charred, scaly honeycomb of his defective cyborg arms. But his stepfather's most terrifying features (Hunter knew them only too well) were hidden for now.

"You're doing a crack job. A *bang-up* job, Hunter," the guardian said, combing his thinning hair with long, ape-like fingers. "I'm proud of you, son. Your mother would be proud, too."

As he appraised Hunter's pale face, the translucent feelers covering his stepfather's body modulated like nerve-endings. He was probing--distrustful--trying to unearth some filial conspiracy against him.

"Clinical trials are a fine way, a *respectable* way to earn a living," the guardian went on. "It's how I met your *sainted* mother. It's how I was able to feed you and your *dear departed* sister, and now that you're a man, you're doing your part and taking your place in our proud family legacy.

"Not everyone is fortunate enough to be able-bodied," the guardian continued, sparking the flint of his lighter repeatedly, a gleam in his jaundiced eye. "Not everyone has been blessed with the *genetic superiority* to use their bodies as currency. Your mother's lineage was hardy, pioneer stock. *True Americans*, strong as oxen, and don't forget it."

The step-father grabbed a newspaper from off the coffee table and handed it to Hunter. The paper advertised the next clinical trial at Celerion. It would implement a surgery that would cut the subject's need for sleep in half. They needed healthy males, the ad said. Aged 18 to 40.

"30 grand for three months," the guardian told him. "I know someone on the board. I'll get you in, Hunter." When he said it the tip of his tongue shot out, licking the delicate bubbles of spittle from between his purple lips.

Hunter tried not to think the words: *Pimp. Devil. Thug.*

The thought of returning to Celerion put his heart in a vice grip. It roped his gut into tight knots. Every molecule in his body contracted against the offense. Hunter folded the advertisement and stuck it into his back pocket.

"It looks like a good one, father. I'll jack in tomorrow. *Register*," he said.

The guardian nodded. Then he fell back asleep in the armchair as quickly as he had woken.

Once outside, Hunter gulped in the night air. He counted, one, two, three, *IN*. Then one, two, three, *OUT*, until his breathing steadied.

He would never go back to Celerion. He would drive. Far away.

Hunter looked down Myrtle Street towards his ticket out.

The broken arm of a dim streetlight cantilevered above the Mustang, swinging idly. Its moody bulb gave the vehicle a flickering, supernatural aura. An army of large tree-roaches marched towards the yellow beast, scurrying in a dark pilgrimage from beneath the rotting foundations of the building. They were an inky, armored river moving under a calm, silver moon. The roaches snaked around the Mustang's heat-cracked tires, and when Hunter opened the driver's door, they scattered all directions like a startled flock: some into the storm drain, some into patches of dead grass, some into rotting balks of timber.

Hunter admired them, perhaps envied them. They were simple, strong survivors.

He took a deep breath, running his hand along the Mustang's cracked dashboard. It was rough and uneven. It was perfect. He checked the visor. No keys. Hunter took the driver's seat and placed his hands on the wheel.

It gave him such a sense of freedom! He imagined the open roads of less than a century ago, and what they must have been like. He had seen them in books and film: wide asphalt veins crisscrossing the land, vehicles speeding along in their lanes like glinting jewels, taking everyone and anyone to all corners of the continent.

Those same interstates had fallen into tectonic disrepair decades ago. (When the affluent citizens took to the air, when the public funds had disappeared.) But Hunter knew that a few choice by-ways were still kept open, bankrolled by rich hobbyists, some even given the lauded title, *National Highway*, to honor the history of the once-prosperous land.

Hunter felt good as he sat in the car. He felt *in accord*. Without thinking, he gave the horn an exploratory push. Its cry rang out through Myrtle Street, blasting him from his reverie. But after a few moments Hunter relaxed again into the womb of the Mustang, seduced by the magic of its moth-eaten upholstery, pulled into hypnotic imaginings of a great, great future:

A vanilla-scented tree hung from the rear-view mirror, and Lila napped in the passenger seat. (Frail, lithe, Lila from Area 5, with her grain-colored skin, and soft, amber lips.) The radio played twentieth-century rock music as they drove the open highway, exploring the ruins of the west.

It was, Hunter felt, *meant to be*. He studied his reflection in the car mirror—his dark eyes, full lips, and thick, raven-black hair. A handsome guy, he thought, and certainly worthy of a beauty such as Lila. Plus, with the *car*. . .

But Hunter's dream ground to a halt. He saw his stepfather's dark figure look on from the stoop, a quiet silhouette rooted there like a black and stunted tree.

Hunter's heart pumped mining sludge. His blood crawled like a lava flow. He recognized a certain complex feeling, as an epileptic recognizes the aura before a seizure.

The guardian's malformed figure came forward into the flickering light and rested against the car's frame.

"Everything okay Hunter? Why are you sitting here, in this yellow car?"

"I have some money left," Hunter said. "And I've always liked autos, father, as you know."

Hunter understood that his words were pointless, but they came automatic, had a mind of their own, ignored reason. The guardian's eyes flashed in the dark street like raccoon eyes.

"Ever since you were four," he agreed, "obsessed with collecting those little cars, those antique *hot wheels*, which your mother hunted down in junk shops, God rest her soul."

"I miss her," Hunter said, gritting his teeth, preparing for the storm.

The stepfather nodded, grunted softly, acknowledging that small piece of Hunter's hurt. Then he began, like always, with the paralysis. Translucent feelers stretched from the guardian's face and slid beneath Hunter's eyelid, through the aqueous fluid, along the smooth muscle, all the way back to the optic nerve, where the appendage interlocked like a terrifying key, opening up a strange new vision.

Hunter imagined the hemispheres of the tyrant's brain lighting up like a pinball machine— an enhanced corpus collosum, Hunter knew, gave his guardian the dreaded psychic abilities.

Hunter was a beetle, pinned to a specimen board.

"Before you leave for Celerion," the stepfather said, "there's a burnt-out motor on the ceiling fan. I'll need your help with that, *son.*"--

The dark script playing out was familiar. There was a disturbed predictability to it that was, in some fucked up way, *comfortable.* Like how the guardian spoke of trivial things as he brutally entered Hunter's mind, as though they were catching up, civilized.

"Motor," Hunter agreed. *"Fan,"* he muttered. The words stuck in his throat like goat heads.

"I'd like all the hangars on the gutters replaced, too. You'll need the hardware for that, of course."

The stepfather spoke in a flat voice, but sent images with teeth:

Hunter's mother consumed by wood rats, laying in a trashed canal. A shimmer of heat. Beetle food. Hunter's body beside her, eyes wide, starting to turn.

A not-so-subtle threat.

Hunter locked in the wine cellar as a young boy. His mother smuggled him a can of white beans. She left behind a trace of perfume and white lace, diaphanous as a ghost. His mother. Ghost. Only the guardian had ever been real. Just the guardian. Always the guardian.

A titan. A mountain. A demon god.

"Good," the stepfather whispered, feeling Hunter's mind buckle, coming to accept his inevitable place in the guardian's ignominious cosmos. . .

A sound of shattering glass broke the otherwise still, dead Myrtle street. The guardian turned to watch as a metal trash bin rolled to a park in the rutted-out pavement near his crime scene.

And for those seconds, the nightmare vibrations broke loose from Hunter's skull. Burned off like an insubstantial fog. Hunter was able to see, at his core, the dense, diamond energy which was his true strength. In a reversal of amplitude, of frequency, a sudden explosion of *yang,* terror turned to bliss. In a vision, the center of Hunter's body irradiated like a small sun.

Not long enough. The guardian turned back, intent as a surgeon on his work.

He showed Hunter the Mustang swallowed by wild grass. Showed him the early days of his passion turn into lassitude and failure. Fluorescent snakes nested in the Mustang's dark wheel wells, and paint-scrawled graffiti-covered its doors. It went to seed. Never meant to be. Swallowed by a piss-colored horizon. . . .

And yet...The guardian was toying with these psychological tactics, waiting with an artist's sense of timing and climax to unleash the grotesque horrors which had, for countless years, kept Hunter in shameful servitude. He could not stand the terrible *waiting*.

Hunter's arm began to burn with a mad-hot pain like frostbite thawing out, and amidst the new, shocking pain in his arm and the fear of what was to come, he realized he had *volition*. He could move it. So he laid into the horn of the Mustang. Hunter screamed with the horn for what seemed forever.

The guardian ate it like sugar. Sucked it up as if through a candy straw. Grew fat on the terrified energy.

Even with the scream of the horn, Myrtle Street stayed dark. It stayed blind, shuttered row- houses. Only New Wife watched in mute complicity from a lighted square of the bedroom window.

But the boys from earlier. The stickball kids. Hunter watched them swagger out from an old service alleyway.

Outside their UV suits, the boys were dressed in soiled, torn clothing, and wore dirty, purple top hats that made them look like thuggish chimney-sweeps. They strutted towards Hunter and the guardian and the streetlight and the car.

In the flickering sulfur light, their green eyes strobed from smut-covered faces. They held bright red cans of coca-cola, the pockets of their jackets heavy with metal jacks, with playing cards, with junkyard swag.

The guardian leaned casually against the car with one arm on its roof. "Hello Billy, Hello Bobby. This is my son Hunter. He was sick," the stepfather told them. "But he's okay now. Tell them you're okay now Hunter."

The guardian spoke to Hunter, but stared at the boys.

They looked past him cynically to Hunter, who sat in the Mustang as white as death.

"We're not idiots," Bobby said.

"Yeah not idiots," Billy echoed. He spat chaw juice onto the ground at the guardian's foot.

For a moment, Hunter saw the guardian through their tough, young eyes: frail, kyphotic, losing his thinning hair in patches. An old man. Not a threat. . .

The guardian's eyes glowered with a mix of bemusement and volatility. "No," he said. "No of course your not *idiots.*"

His amused expression turned cold and the guardian's smile spread. It spread so wide it shattered his face into horrible bloody rifts, into monstrous, skin-fractured puzzle pieces. The streetlight threw sulfur sparks in some kind of electric introduction, and under the night's full moon and the chemical storm, the guardian transmogrified.

The demon had a bent, sick body like a crook-backed giant. It moved awkwardly on muscular, lice-infested goat legs. Twenty pairs of dark pit-eyes blinked from its cryptic skull. Its monstrous face was covered in long, white hairs which modulated in the moonlight like waves of white, silky grain. A murderous horn pushed through the demon's forehead, ripping skull and flesh, and membranous black wings unfolded from its ridged back.

As quickly as reptile tongues, rope-like feelers reached from the demon's mange-coated body. The feelers struck out for the boys, yet once they found their fleeing legs, the tacky appendages continued without urgency, viscous fingers crawling up their calves, their thighs, their backs, and knocking their hats onto the street to cradle their skulls in a strange, vascular headdress.

As Hunter watched the horror unfold he shut down. An unbelievable fatigue, blood deep and abysmal, demolished him. His body was tapped out. It had no adrenaline left to give. As the world browned at its edges, Hunter felt a surge of gratitude that he might escape into some dark and dreamless sleep, as he had escaped on so many countless black nights during childhood.

But he awoke (minutes, hours?) later. Billy and Bobby sat beside Hunter in the Mustang. Their top-hats were crookedly back in place, their rangy bodies crammed into the narrow passenger seat, oddly buckled in. The boys stared a thousand miles through the windshield. They gripped their red coke cans like lifeless wax figurines, all set for some demonic road trip.

In the rearview mirror, Hunter watched the guardian demon spread its dark wings like a terrifying angel. It blotted out the stars and the moon. Storm clouds roiled above them, pouring forth a torrential, black rain over Myrtle Street.

In the storm's downdrafts, the Mustang shook and bucked in a horrible metallic disharmony. It slowly filled with foul rainwater, as if the vehicle was sinking into a dank, clogged river.

But Hunter could end it. Give himself over completely. Save the boys.

The demon only killed when terror failed, as it had finally failed with Hunter's mother, with his sister, and with countless others. Only Hunter had stayed the long and shameful course.

The guardian needed Hunter. Needed his *dollars*. His *earning power*. His filial servitude.

All it required was submission.

Hunter turned to the strange, child-sized manikins in the seat beside him.

"I'm all better now," he whispered. "I'm not sick anymore," he told them. "My father is taking me to the hospital."

Magic, childish words. Even his voice took on the treble tones of young, frightened innocence, the tone of telling secrets in the dim shine of nightlight.

Hunter saw the Celerion compound in his mind's eye, raking the bruised sky, rising up from the valley floor like a steel mountain. Celerion had always been there. Since the earth had been loose rock hurtling through space, since before the sun. Since before the galaxies had spun out from their unimaginable pinpoint of density.

Destiny.

The compound waiting for Hunter's body like a hungry beast.

He accepted it as his home.

He accepted the guardian as his father. His dark king.

Hunter sat in the Mustang, panting.

The passenger seat was empty.

The lightening sky silent.

The guardian gone.

Water ran off the street in peaceful eddies, carving rivulets into the baked dirt.

Hunter crawled onto the pavement and lay on his back, staring into the sky as the lighted windows of his stepfather's home became shuttered eyes. It might have been hours before the dogs of light raced past him.

There were so many more than Hunter remembered! Flooding Myrtle street, clogging it with their radiance. And just when it seemed as though they had forgotten him, would leave him lying there in the street, the dogs turned back in recognition, stampeding their starlight. Tears streamed down Hunter's cheeks. He was happy, *so happy*, for this reunion. The dogs pawed Hunter with large, clumsy feet. They licked him with firework tongues like Roman candles. Their ecstatic tails could never hide the immense love they felt for him.

The End.

Mary Renzi

Mary Renzi's fiction has appeared or is forthcoming from Hypnos, One Throne, Pantheon, Zymbol, decomP, Space Squid, Deadly Chaps, and a bunch of other cool places. She writes for Dirge Magazine.

Hello horror lover.
If you've been suffering from a persistent desire
for just a little more unpleasantness in your life,
we have the answer:
NOCTURNAL
TRANSMISSIONS
PODCAST
Nocturnal Transmissions is a fortnightly podcast featuring
inspired performances of dark tales both old and new
by voice artist Kristin Holland.
Find them at
nocturnaltransmissions.com.au
or wherever good podcasts are purveyed.

If you have any feedback or would like to leave a review please head over to Amazon and share your thoughts about Sanitarium.

Thank you for your time and we salute your love for all things horror.

https://www.facebook.com/SanitariumPublishing

https://www.thesanitarium.co.uk/

https://twitter.com/sanitariumlit

https://www.instagram.com/sanitariumpublishing/